Amy Cross is the author of more than 100 horror, paranormal, fantasy and thriller novels.

OTHER TITLES
BY AMY CROSS INCLUDE

American Coven
Annie's Room
The Ash House
Asylum
B&B
The Bride of Ashbyrn House
The Camera Man
The Curse of Wetherley House
The Devil, the Witch and the Whore
Devil's Briar
The Dog
Eli's Town
The Farm
The Ghost of Molly Holt
The Ghosts of Lakeforth Hotel
The Girl Who Never Came Back
Haunted
The Haunting of Blackwych Grange
Like Stones on a Crow's Back
The Night Girl
Perfect Little Monsters & Other Stories
Stephen
The Shades
The Soul Auction
Tenderling
Ward Z

THE GHOST OF BRIARWYCH CHURCH

AMY CROSS

This collected edition
first published by Dark Season Books,
United Kingdom, 2018

ISBN: 9781790855858

Also available in e-book format.

www.amycross.com

CONTENTS

Prologue
PAGE 15

Chapter One
PAGE 27

Chapter Two
PAGE 31

Chapter Three
PAGE 39

Chapter Four
PAGE 45

Chapter Five
PAGE 51

Chapter Six
PAGE 61

Chapter Seven
PAGE 71

Chapter Eight
PAGE 79

Chapter Nine
PAGE 87

Chapter Ten
PAGE 97

Chapter Eleven
page 107

Chapter Twelve
page 115

Chapter Thirteen
page 125

Chapter Fourteen
page 133

Chapter Fifteen
page 143

Chapter Sixteen
page 153

Chapter Seventeen
page 167

Chapter Eighteen
page 181

Chapter Nineteen
page 187

Chapter Twenty
page 213

Chapter Twenty-one
page 241

Chapter Twenty-two
PAGE 251

Chapter Twenty-three
PAGE 265

Chapter Twenty-four
PAGE 270

Epilogue
PAGE 273

THE GHOST OF BRIARWYCH CHURCH

PROLOGUE

Many years ago

"WHAT DO *YOU* WANT to be when you grow up, Judith?" Prue asks as she walks a little way ahead, leading me along a path that follows the bend of the stream. "A school matron, maybe?"

"I don't know," I reply, feeling mildly irritated by the question. "I suppose for now I'll just clean houses, like my mother does."

"What about a husband?" Prue continues, turning and grinning at me. "You do want a husband, don't you? Or do you want to be an old maid?"

"I'm in no hurry," I tell her. "Nor should you be. At the age of fifteen, a girl should be concentrating on her studies."

"Of course," she says. "Nobody wants to be a wet blanket, do they? But everyone wants a husband. How would you live without one?"

She laughs and continues walking, which at least is a blessed relief. I don't know why I even agreed to come out here with her. Actually, that's not true. I *do* know why. I came because my mother pressured me. She complained that I spend too much time studying scripture, and she thinks I need to get out into the world and make some friends. I've tried telling her that I'll make friends when I meet some interesting people, but she thinks I should persevere with the likes of Prudence Williams. The problem is that girls such as Prudence are so boring, and so fixated on trivial matters such as boys and nice dresses.

"Hey, what's this?" Prue says suddenly, stopping ahead and reaching down.

I spot something glinting in the grass, and I watch as she holds up what appears to be a beautiful silver necklace.

"Someone must have dropped it," she continues, turning to me. "Isn't it pretty?"

"It is," I reply, stepping closer and marveling at the light that catches on the sides of a small silver crucifix that's dangling from the chain. "It's one of the most beautiful things I've ever seen."

"Well, it's mine," Prue says, opening the necklace and slipping it around her neck. "I found it."

"It must belong to someone," I tell her. "We should ask when we get home."

"Whoever it *used* to belong to, they clearly didn't care for it enough to look after it." She adjusts the necklace and then she grins at me. "It's mine now. I think it looks really pretty on me. Don't you?"

"It does," I reply through gritted teeth. "Although, you don't go to church much, do you? So why would you want a necklace like that?"

"Because it's pretty," she says, rolling her eyes and then turning to walk away. "What other reason could there be? Not everything has to be about bloody churches all the time, Judith."

***

Several hours later, sitting on the grass in Sutter's Meadow, I watch the distant spire of Briarwych Church rising above the English countryside. Today is an exceptionally hot day, hotter than any I have ever known, and I must confess that I am rather sweating.

"It's boiling," Prue says, with a hint of a whine in her voice. "This must be the hottest day on record, surely."

"We should be careful in the sun," I remind her. "We don't want to burn."

"I don't mind. In fact -"

Suddenly she puts her arms over her head, and I watch in horror as she removes her dress.

"What are you doing?" I gasp.

"Relax, there's no-one around to see," she says, setting her dress down and then grinning at me. She's wearing only her underwear now. "You're so buttoned-up, Judith, and you're sweating so. Why don't you take a leaf out of my book and cool down? It might even do you some good to get a little tanned. You're always so freakishly white."

"I have a sensitive complexion!" I tell her, but she's already settling down on her back and closing her eyes.

"The sun is good for one's health."

"So is proper dress."

"I love the warmth of the sun on my body," she explains. "Oh, I feel like one of those rich ladies who can afford to go to the south of France every summer. If I had a husband who could pay for me to do that, I think I'd go all the time. I do love England, but I think I belong somewhere a little warmer. Now, if I could bag myself one of those husbands who has a villa down near the Mediterranean, I think I would be set for life. I really don't see what other ambition any woman could possibly have."

I glance around, just to make sure that nobody is nearby. It would be frightfully improper if someone chanced upon us now and saw Prue in her under-garments. Indeed, it's frightfully improper with just the two of us here. I watch the treeline for a moment, to see whether there might be anybody lurking in the darkness. For a few seconds I feel as if perhaps we *are* being watched, but there's clearly nobody out there. I keep watching, however, as I wipe sweat from my brow.

"Don't you ever tire of being such a prude?" Prue asks, and I turn to see that she has her eyes closed, with her head turned to the left. She looks almost as if she's on the verge of going to sleep. "You must be so hot in all that wool. Isn't the sweat just dribbling all over the place?"

"I'm quite alright," I tell her, although I must admit that I can feel dampness under my armpits and at the backs of my knees.

"If you say so," she murmurs. "I know I couldn't live the way you do. I prefer to..."

Her voice trails off.

"I prefer..."

And then she's gone. I swear, I can pinpoint the exact moment at which she falls asleep, and a moment later – as if to confirm my suspicions – she begins to snore.

As I wipe more sweat from my brow, and from the sides of my face as well, my attention is caught by another glint of light from the silver crucifix that now rests just past Prue's collarbone.

That necklace really is a thing of beauty, and I feel rather angry that it is now the property of such a brazen, irreligious rascal as Prudence Williams. Such a fine crucifix should be owned by somebody who appreciates not only its beauty, but also its meaning.

I wipe more sweat away, as beads start dribbling down my face and onto my neck. I can feel more sweat under my clothes now, and it is as if the temperature is increasing steadily with each passing second.

Letting out a faint gasp, I turn and look out across the field. A haze of heat is rising from the ground, obscuring the view of Briarwych. Indeed, the heat is now so strong, I am beginning to feel rather nauseous. I wipe more and more sweat from my face, but it is almost as if I am burning up, as if this beautiful English field is becoming as hot as the surface of the sun. I turn my head this way and that, trying to shield my face from the brightness, and then – feeling once again as if I am being watched – I look toward the treeline. There is nobody there, yet I feel a pair of eyes burning into my soul.

"This is quite impossible," I gasp, looking down at Prue and seeing that somehow she is still sleeping through the heat, still snoring too.

And the crucifix is still glinting.

"I've never known such a day," I whisper, wondering if perhaps the pair of us are to be burned to scorch-marks out here in the field. I turn and look around, and suddenly I spot something on the ground near my right foot.

A rock.

I didn't notice it before, but there is a large black rock that seems not to fit at all with the rest of the countryside. About as large as a human head, the rock looks to be glistening in the heat. Reaching out, I touch the hot surface and find that, indeed, the rock is slightly damp.

Filled with a sense of wonder, I take the rock in my hands, even though the surface is almost burning my skin.

A moment later, turning to Prue, I feel a sudden rush of blood as I realize that I could use this rock to just *take* the crucifix. In fact, I am starting to wonder whether this is a test from the Lord, whether it is my duty to ensure that the necklace does not become the property of such a weak and foolish girl. Still gripping the rock, I try to clear my thoughts, but it is as if the immense heat is slowly boiling my brain in my skull. My mind is slow and turgid, and I barely feel like myself.

Finally, gasping for air, I turn and kneel next to Prue. I feel as if my brain is turning to mush, but then I raise the rock in my hands and the heat seems to ease slightly. I raise the rock higher and, again, the heat becomes a little more bearable. I can still feel sweat soaking under my clothes, but as I keep rock raised high I at least gain a short respite. Only for a few seconds, however, for soon the heat begins once again to build.

"Please," I whisper, "I can't stand this."

And then, with no warning, I am suddenly filled with the understanding that the heat will fade as soon as I bring the rock crashing down against Prue's head. Yes, that's the only thing that'll do it. The heat will fade, I shall stop burning with sweat, and I shall be able to take the necklace as my own. Nobody will find Prue's body out here in the middle of the field, not before it's eaten by animals, and I can make up some lie about where she's gone. I can say that she went to visit friends, and then people will forget to ask again later. Yes, that seems perfectly reasonable. This is the only course of action that will allow me to stay sane.

With all my strength, I suddenly bring the rock crashing down against Prue's head. I see and hear and feel her skull cracking with a dull thud. She doesn't wake up. Her body jerks slightly, but I'm already raising the rock again. This time, I bring it down against her eye, obliterating the socket and sending blood splattering out across the grass. I raise the rock yet again and watch for a moment as more blood bursts out from between broken sheets of bone, and then I smash the rock over and over against Prue's face until all that is left is a bloodied mess. Then I keep going, aiming at the top of her neck, hitting her and not even caring when blood sprays against my face. I work myself into a frenzy, bashing her head until finally my hands seize up and I drop the rock, and I see that I have bashed Prue's head clear away from her shoulders.

With trembling fingers, I carefully reach out and touch the crucifix. It's burning hot and -

"Judith, what are you doing?"

Startled, I blink, and suddenly my hands are free of blood. I look over at the spot where Judith's head used to be, and I'm shocked to see her staring at me with a puzzled expression.

"If you like the necklace that much," she continues, "you can have it. You only had to say."

I pull my hands away, and then I look around and see that there is indeed a black rock resting on the ground. The heat has begun to abate, and after a few more seconds the air is once again quite bearable. The day remains hot, of course, but at least the startling intensity has faded quite dramatically.

"Here," Prue says, sitting up and removing the necklace, then holding it out for me. "It'll suit you better anyway. It'll mean more to you."

"I'm fine," I stammer, as I realize that I must have imagined that whole dreadful business with the rock. It seemed so real, but it must have been all in my head.

"You don't *look* fine," Prue continues,

before pressing the hot little metal crucifix into my hands and then grabbing her dress. "Did I fall asleep? Must be the heat. How about going somewhere a little more shady?"

As she begins to get dressed again, I look down at the crucifix. I am quite shaken by the realization that I actually contemplated murdering Prue in order to get my hands on this thing, and by the fact that I was able to imagine – in such great detail – what it would be like to smash her brains out with a rock. Never before have I felt myself to be remotely capable of violent acts, yet evidently today some long-hidden part of my personality briefly came bubbling to the surface. I must never, ever let that happen again.

"I fancy a walk through the forest on the way back to Briarwych," Prue says, as I get to my feet. "We can go and pick bluebells like proper, dainty women. Sound fun?"

"Yes," I stammer, still contemplating the bizarre, animal-like fury that briefly blossomed in my heart. "Of course."

"Last one there's a scaredy-cat," she says, turning and heading toward the treeline. "Come on, Judith. Let's get a move on!"

Still clutching the crucifix, I turn to follow her, only to stop as I see that she's heading straight for the darkness of the forest. For a moment I feel once again as if I am being watched, but I quickly tell myself that this sensation is all in my head. Setting off after Prue, I try to make myself believe that the hallucination was perfectly innocent, although I know deep down that this is not true. When I get home, I shall have to pray for guidance from the Lord, and I must devote myself more carefully than ever to scripture studies. If some kind of evil truly lurks within my soul, I must beg the Lord to help me keep it hidden.

I want to live a good and holy life.

CHAPTER ONE

1940

I AM THE LUCKIEST, happiest, most content woman in the whole world.

As I step out of the cottage, I look – as I always do – to the left and see the spire of Briarwych Church rising high above our splendid little village. There is something so noble about that spire, something that fills my heart with joy. One should always appreciate a church, of course, but I must say I think there is something a little different about Briarwych. It is as if all that is good is here, and nothing bad could ever intrude upon this perfection.

"Good morning, Ms. Prendergast," a friendly voice calls out, and I turn to see Millicent

Bean heading down the hill, no doubt on her way to the local shop.

"Good morning, Mrs. Bean," I reply, as I wave at her. "I was just enjoying the warmth of the morning sunshine against my face."

"Indeed, Ms. Prendergast," she says, as she disappears from view behind my neighbor's rose bushes. "I shall speak to you later, I hope."

"I hope so too," I reply, although I imagine she is already well out of earshot. That woman is always rushing around and I sometimes wonder whether she ever has time to contemplate the peace and quiet of Briarwych.

Then again, one should not judge one's neighbors.

I pull the front door shut, before making my way along the garden path and out onto the lane. As I shut the gate, I glance up at the clear blue sky and note that there is not a cloud in sight. Even by Briarwych standards, this is shaping up to be a particularly bright and sunny day, and I cannot help but wonder what great purpose the Lord has in store for me today. More than anything, I like to feel truly useful to the church and its community, and I trust that the Lord knows how best to use me. On a day such as this, I cannot help but feel that something truly wonderful is about to happen.

With this thought prominent in my mind, I start making my way up the hill. It would be unladylike to go too fast, but I cannot help quickening my pace as I once again spot the church's spire up ahead. I have so much work to get done today, so I must get started as quickly as possible. As all good people know, the Lord abhors idleness, and I personally believe that one must at all times strive to maximize the usefulness of one's time. And if one is fortunate, one might find oneself being put to work as an instrument of the Lord.

Yes, I truly *am* the luckiest woman in the world.

CHAPTER TWO

"GOOD MORNING, FATHER PERKINS."

"Hmm?"

Turning from the papers on his desk, Father Perkins stares at me for a moment. He is a very hard worker, and he is often too engrossed in his tasks to notice my arrival. This I take to the mark of a serious and devoted man who perhaps becomes a little lost in his work from time to time.

"Oh," he mutters, as he looks back at the papers, "good morning, Judith. You're even earlier than usual, I see. By a good half hour this time. There's really no need to hurry in the mornings, you know."

"I thought I'd rearrange the hymn books first," I tell him. "I'm afraid people just don't treat them with the proper respect, and some are rather dog-eared. If I put the dog-eared copies toward the back, people will -"

"That sounds very good, Judith," Father Perkins replies, interrupting me and sounding rather as if he is once again preoccupied with his writing. "Whatever floats your boat."

Before I can reply, I spot the latest newspaper on his desk. I try not to read the news very much at the moment, on account of all the terrible stories about the war. I prefer to content myself with the hope – no, the belief – that the Lord will see us through these dark days and that eventually we shall triumph. How could we not? And we must maintain our way of life, as best we can, while we wait for the darkness to pass.

"I would really like to order some new books," I say, "with a few more rigorous hymns included. As I have suggested before, Father, the current books contains a few frivolous texts that I do not believe are really suitable for our work here at the church."

"People don't seem to mind too much, Judith," he murmurs.

"It's still important," I remind him, and I must admit that I'm a little shocked by his nonchalance. "I know the budget is rather over-stretched," I add, hoping to strike a conciliatory tone. "I'm sure we can make do with what we have, once the covers have been suitably cleaned. And glued in places. And cut in others, to get rid of crude annotations. And had their spines repaired."

I wait for him to reply, but instead he simply turns to another page and continues with his work. I know he's not being rude, of course; he's simply a very focused man, and I respect that quality tremendously. With a faint smile, I turn and head back out into the corridor and then I make my way toward the shelf where the hymn books are kept. I am greatly looking forward to another quiet day of hard work.

"David, are you here?" a shrill voice calls out, and I flinch as I hear footsteps hurrying into the church.

Even before I turn to look, I know that Violet Durridge is here for another of her increasingly frequent meetings. Tottering into the church on high heels, and with make-up plastered all over her face, she looks – as usual – like the most deplorable sort of irreligious wastrel. It's a wonder she has managed to tear herself away from her favorite bar stool in the local pub. She even has a cigarette in one hand, and she has not extinguished the tip before coming into the church. Some people simply have no decorum whatsoever.

"Hello Judith," she says, glancing briefly at me before heading through to Father Perkins' office. "Nice day, isn't it?"

"It was," I reply, although I quickly

admonish myself.

I should be more charitable. Violet Durridge has faced challenges in her life and she is a human being, like the rest of us. It is not my place to judge. I shall leave that to a higher power.

"Violet," I hear Father Perkins say warmly, followed by the sound of his chair-legs scraping as he gets to his feet. "What a lovely surprise. I wasn't expecting you to come back so soon."

Nor was I.

Her visits are becoming irritatingly frequent.

"You know I can't stay away for long," she says with her typical bubbly glee. "I just wanted to make sure that you haven't forgotten our tombola plans. You'll be pleased to know that several ladies have already confirmed their interest."

"That's wonderful," Father Perkins replies. "Your tombolas always bring the church to life in the most magnificent manner. In fact, I'd go so far as to say that they're an integral part of the fabric of Briarwych village life."

"As are you, Father," she says. "By the way, I hope you've had time to think about my offer. You know I'd be only too happy to do some light cleaning for you. A woman without a husband is, of course, always hoping to help others, and I wouldn't like there to be too much strain on poor Ms. Prendergast's shoulders. Not when she already has a daughter to look after. As an unwed mother, of course, she surely has far too much on her plate."

Fighting against my dislike for the woman, I pick up some hymn books and carry them through the arched doorway, hoping to find a quiet spot where Violet's voice won't seem so loud and penetrating.

"Not all of us single ladies are like that dusty old Judith Prendergast," Violet adds, a little more quietly now. "I saw her as I came in. My word, the woman's a prude, isn't she?"

Stopping, I feel a slow, seething anger start to rise through my body, although I quickly remind myself once again that I must rise above such things.

"I don't know how she can act all holier-than-thou all the time," she continues. "I mean, the woman had a child out of wedlock! That's not exactly respectable behavior, is it?"

Closing my eyes, I find myself having to try harder and harder to stay calm. There is – I must confess – a part of me that wants to go through and give Violet Durridge a piece of my mind.

"Judith Prendergast is an asset to this church," Father Perkins explains.

That's better.

"And you enjoy her company, do you?" Violet asks.

"So tell me some more about this month's tombola," Father Perkins replies, conspicuously failing to defend me. "Will you be using the same arrangements as before, or are you planning on trying those new elements that you mentioned to me last time?"

"You know me, Father. I always like to mix things up."

"That is an admirable quality," he says, sounding genuinely enthused. "In these times, we must remember to keep our minds working."

Preferring to not hear any of this inane chatter, I carry the hymn books to the front pew and set them down, and then I kneel to pray. Any time I feel myself losing control, I turn to the Lord so that I can receive some guidance. I know that there is wickedness within my soul, but I also know that I can control this wickedness through prayer and contemplation.

"Dear Lord," I whisper as I put my hands together, close my eyes and bow my head, "give me the strength to not look down upon others. I should be more compassionate and less vain. Give me the strength to love all people and to never judge them. Not even Violet Durridge."

I wait, hoping that the Lord will have heard me.

"I am sorry," I continue finally. "Sometimes my thoughts overtake me. I try so hard to follow your teachings, but there are times when some inner part of my soul seems to reach up and..."

I pause as I try to work out exactly how to describe the sensation.

"I am sure that you understand," I say after a few seconds. "You understand all. Amen."

I make the sign of the cross against my chest.

"Would you like me to do something about that woman?" a female voice asks suddenly.

Startled, I open my eyes and look around, but there is no sign of anybody nearby. I can just about hear Father Perkins and Violet still talking in the office, yet there is quite clearly nobody close to me. Nevertheless, as I get to my feet, I am quite certain that the voice was real. I take a look along the nearest pews, and then I head up the steps and look behind the altar, but I am absolutely alone.

Yet that voice seemed so real.

"Hello?" I say cautiously, although I feel rather foolish as I continue to look around.

Turning, I half expect someone to leap out and admit that they have played a cruel trick on me, but there really is nobody around. How I heard that voice, I cannot begin to imagine, but I must assume that my ears deceived me. Perhaps I suffered a momentary lapse that allowed me to conjure up that voice. In fact, that is the only reasonable explanation.

I must admit, I feel a little flustered as I sit down and start sorting out the hymn books.

Meanwhile, in the distance, Father Perkins and Violet Durridge are laughing about something.

CHAPTER THREE

"DO I HAVE TO go to school tomorrow?" Elizabeth asks as she continues to dry the dishes from dinner. "I'd much rather stay at home and help you."

"Your education is important," I tell her.

"It doesn't *seem* important," she replies. "Why do I need to know about history, or about mathematics? Why do I need to be able to multiply seven by eight? What good will that ever do me?"

"No man wants a simpleton for a wife," I explain. "You never know when these things will come in handy."

"And who says that I want to be a wife?"

"What exactly is your alternative proposition?"

"I don't know, but I'd like to keep my

options open."

Glancing at her, I see that she's serious. I can't help smiling at her determination.

"You'll see as you get older," I tell her. "Your priorities will change and you'll come to value the love of a good man. I suppose in the future women will want everything to be equal. Myself, I'm not sure how that will work. It is better in this life to have a place, and to know that place, and to occupy that place fully. A life spent constantly in search of a place would seem, to me, to be absolute torture."

I wait for her to admit that I'm right. After finishing scrubbing the saucepan, however, I turn and see that Elizabeth looks rather upset. Indeed, I rather fear that there are tears in her eyes.

"Did it happen again?" I ask, as I feel a flicker of cold anger in my chest.

"It's nothing," she replies, sniffing back more tears. "I shouldn't let it bother me."

"I thought this was resolved," I say with a sigh. "Elizabeth, this has been going on for so long now. I shall have to speak again to your headmaster and -"

"No, don't do that!" she blurts out. "That only made it worse last time!"

"Those girls are little monsters," I continue. "How dare they mock you, just because..."

My voice trails off for a moment as I see a

single tear trickle down Elizabeth's face. She wipes it away quickly enough, but then another falls and she turns away so that I can't see the rest.

"Your father was a good man," I tell her, as I have told her on countless occasions before. "Yes, you were born out of wedlock, and that *is* a sin. It is one of only two times in my life when I have gone against my better judgment. We were young and foolish, and we couldn't help ourselves." I pause, before stepping up behind her and putting a hand on her shoulder. "But I wouldn't change anything," I continue, "and I wouldn't apologize to anyone, because without that night I would not be blessed with you, my darling. And I promise that if your father hadn't been killed in that car accident, he would have married me before the bump even began to show."

I wait, but I can hear her still sniffling.

"Nobody has the right to mock you for any of this," I add, "and it breaks my heart to see you like this. I know I have a reputation as a rather prim woman, and people like to knock others off their pedestals. But next time somebody makes fun of you, tell them to come and see me instead, and I shall give them a piece of my mind. Before you complain, I might remind you that I am your mother and that it is my duty to worry about you."

"Might I be excused?" she asks.

"Are you going to go and cry in your

room?"

"I have some homework that I must do."

"Let me see your face first."

She hesitates, and then she turns to me, and I immediately see the tears shimmering in her reddened eyes. Her bottom lip is trembling, and I can tell that she is struggling to keep from sobbing.

"Elizabeth," I say with a sigh, "let me -"

"I'm sorry!" she gasps, and then she turns and hurries away.

Left standing alone in the kitchen, I flinch as I hear her bedroom door swing shut. I want to wring the necks of those stupid schoolgirls who taunt my daughter, but I know I shall have to simply go and speak to the headmaster again. This terrible behavior must stop. Of course, deep down I know that none of this is Elizabeth's fault. It is my fault. Elizabeth suffers because I am her mother. She has always suffered from that association. The entire village looks down on us, even if they are usually friendly to our faces.

Suddenly I hear her door open again, and she hurries back through.

"Mother, have you seen outside?" she asks, her eyes now filled with shock. "I think a cottage is on fire down the road!"

***

"Get out of the way!" a man shouts at the end of the lane, as Elizabeth and I hurry along to join the group that has gathered to watch. "Move on!"

Elizabeth was right. Flames are roaring from the upper level of one of the cottages. Set against the night sky, the flames seem particularly bright, and I can hear the roar of the fire as it tears through the building. And as men rush back and forth with buckets, I suddenly realize that the cottage on the end of the row is the one that Muriel Agerton used to own, and which was sold just a year ago to...

"Violet Durridge," I whisper, watching as the flames leap high into the darkness.

"That's Violet's house, isn't it?" Elizabeth says. "Mother, she'll be alright, won't she?"

"Has anyone seen Violet?" a man calls out nearby. "When was the last time she was out?"

"She was in the pub earlier," another man says, "but she said she was going home about two hours ago!"

"This is dreadful," Elizabeth continues, and I turn to see light from the flames flickering against her face. "Mother, Ms. Durridge wouldn't still be in there, would she? She'd have left as soon as she noticed the flames!"

"She was pretty drunk when she left," one of the men mutters nearby. "I saw her stumbling out of the pub, barely able to stand. She had a cigarette in her mouth, too. I almost offered to walk her home but, well, we all tend to avoid that on account of how our wives don't like it. Violet can get a little overbearing sometimes, if you know what I mean."

"But she can't actually be in there, can she?" Elizabeth asks, as if the thought is too horrific to comprehend. "It's just not possible."

I want to reassure her but, as I continue to watch the flames, I can't help thinking back to the voice I heard earlier in the church. The voice can't have been real, of course, yet it's certainly a coincidence that I would have imagined such a thing just a few short hours before Violet's house went up in flames.

I can only hope that somehow, by some miracle, she is not in those flames right now.

CHAPTER FOUR

STEPPING OUT OF THE gate, I look along the lane and immediately see that several vehicles are parked outside the remains of Violet's house. The fire was eventually put out during the night, but now – as I make my way along the lane – I'm shocked to see the sheer ferocity of the damage that has left Violet's home almost completely destroyed. The lower floor seems relatively intact, but the upper floor has been wrecked.

Hearing voices nearby, I turn just in time to see two men carrying a stretcher out of the building. There's a white sheet covering something on the stretcher, and somehow I immediately understand that this is a human body.

"Is it her?" a woman whispers nearby, and I turn to see the fear in her eyes. "Oh, poor Violet.

They say she was smoking in bed, and that she was drunk so she fell asleep. It's just awful to think about!"

"Indeed," I reply, before looking back toward the stretcher as the men start to load it into the back of an ambulance. "One can only hope that she -"

Suddenly a strong gust of wind blows along the lane, and the white sheet is ripped away from the stretcher. In that instant, I am horrified to see Violet Durridge's body. Or rather, what is *left* of the body. Her flesh has been almost entirely burned away, and my eyes are instantly drawn to her skull, which is turned slightly to one side with the mouth partially open. Her hands, meanwhile, are held up close to her face, as if she was trying to get away from the flames when she died. She certainly does not appear to be in the position of a woman in her sleep.

The men quickly recover the body and finish loading it into the ambulance, and then they slam the door shut.

***

"It is quite awful," Father Perkins says as we sit in his office, each with a cup of tea. "To think that this time yesterday she was in here, laughing and joking, and now she's..."

His voice trails off, and it's clear that he's in shock.

“I warned her about the drink,” I say after a moment. “Many people did. I hear she was at the public house last night and, well, apparently she was not entirely sober by the time she left.”

“She certainly lived life to the full.”

“Perhaps she went a little too far,” I suggest. “A sip of port or brandy at Christmas is one thing. Perpetual licentiousness is quite another.”

“One should not speak ill of the dead, Judith.”

“But one should learn from their mistakes,” I point out.

“I know, I know,” he replies, interrupting me. “At least she was probably asleep when it happened. She probably didn't feel anything.”

“Actually,” I say, “I saw the -”

I stop myself just in time. One does not need to always be too open about these things, and I suppose I should not force Father Perkins to consider the unsavory truth. Looking down at my cup of tea, I try to think of something more appropriate that I might say, but then I glance at the doorway and spot the altar at the other end of the church. For a few seconds, I think back to the voice that I heard yesterday, and I feel a flicker of unease as I remember its very specific comment about poor Violet Durridge.

"Have you ever heard anything in here?" I ask, turning back to Father Perkins.

"Such as?"

"I hesitate to even say," I continue, worried that I shall sound like a lunatic. I pause, and then I smile and shake my head. "Never mind. The mind can play such dreadful tricks on one, can it not?"

"I suppose so," he replies with a sigh. "I shall have to start work on what I'm to say at Violet's funeral. The poor woman didn't have any family, you know. Not anyone close, at least. Of course, I'll take on the responsibility of arranging everything. She'll be given a spot in the cemetery and I shall personally arrange for a headstone to be erected. She might have been a rather controversial figure in the village, but Violet was a well-known member of the community and we have a duty to take care of our own."

"You are a good man," I tell him.

"I do my best."

"No, you are a *truly* good man," I continue, keen to make him understand. "I watch you work sometimes, Father, and I am constantly amazed by the way you dedicate yourself to this church." I pause for a moment, watching his expression as he stares down at his cup. "It's especially impressive," I add cautiously, "in light of the fact that you are unmarried. I would have thought that a man in your position would be quite keen to take a wife. To have somebody who can support you and help you. Guide you. Look after you."

"You might have a point," he says, sounding distracted. "I'm always too busy to go courting. I've never really got into all that."

"Perhaps you should."

"And who should I marry?" he asks, before shaking his head. "I'm fine, Judith. Really. I get by."

"Love comes in many forms," I tell him. "Perhaps it could be right under your nose and you have only to -"

"I should get on with things," he says suddenly, getting to his feet and drinking the rest of his tea, before setting the cup down. "Thank you so much for that, Judith, you've been a great help. If anybody comes to see me, perhaps in search of guidance after this terrible tragedy, be sure to show them through, won't you?"

"Of course," I say, as I realize that – for now – the moment has passed and there shall be no more talk of marriage. Perhaps I should have waited to bring it up, but I have waited so long already. Father Perkins is a wise man, but in this one particular aspect he has a blind-spot; he does not see that the answer to all his problems is sitting here in the room with him.

As I stand, I try to think of something else I might say, something that could offer a little comfort to Father Perkins at this difficult time. Finally, however, I tell myself that he must be left to work in peace.

Once I am out of the office, I head to the kitchen and get on with some light work. In my mind's eye, I keep replaying the moment earlier when the sheet blew away from the stretcher, when I saw Violet Durridge's burned body. People are saying that she hopefully died without waking, but the body I saw seemed twisted into the most horrendous scream and I am afraid I cannot lie to myself. I believe she woke as she burned, I believe she knew exactly what was happening to her. I believe her death must have been truly horrific.

I cannot prevent a faint smile from curling on my lips.

CHAPTER FIVE

"HOW WAS SCHOOL TODAY, Elizabeth?"

I watch her face for any hint of trouble, but this time she does not even look at me. Her cutlery bumps against the plate for a moment as she continues to eat her dinner, and it is as if she is having to think of the right answer.

"It was fine, Mother," she says eventually.

"Was there any more trouble?"

"There was no trouble."

"That's good." I pause, finding this story a little difficult to believe. After all, I have seen those cackling schoolgirls on many occasions before, and they do not seem to be the type of people who would simply withdraw their claws without prompting. "And the difficulties of yesterday are truly resolved?"

"They are."

"Did you speak to the headmaster, Elizabeth?"

"No."

"Then -"

"It's just fine," she says, interrupting me. "There's nothing to discuss, Mother. I should rather eat and then go through to do my homework." Finally she glances at me, but only briefly, before looking back down at her food. I can tell that she is hesitant. "There is nothing to discuss."

"I see," I reply.

She's lying.

I know my daughter and I know when she's lying. She must have been bullied again today at school, most likely by those same girls who have been tormenting her of late. She is simply too good-hearted and too kind to let me know. She wants me to not worry, yet here I sit in a state of great distress. I really must cycle over to the school some time and have a word with that idle headmaster who seems not to notice what goes on in his own classrooms.

"She didn't go to school today," a female voice whispers suddenly.

I freeze.

It is the same voice that I heard yesterday in the church, the same voice that spoke about Violet Durridge. I had just about convinced myself that the voice was a brief, imagined thing, but now it is here again. Am I losing my mind?

"She is making the same mistake that you once made," the voice continues, as I watch Elizabeth eat. "The exact same mistake, as it happens. If you don't believe me, look in her school bag. You won't like what you find."

"I -"

Catching myself just in time, I realize I cannot possibly answer the voice. If I start talking to myself out-loud, I shall certainly seem rather peculiar.

Elizabeth glances at me.

"Were you going to say something, Mother?"

I swallow hard. Quite evidently, she did not herself hear the voice.

"Are you alright?" she asks, furrowing her brow. "You look a little pale and worried."

"I'm fine," I tell her. "Finish your peas."

She starts eating again, but I merely sit rigidly in my chair and wait in case the voice returns. As the minutes pass, however, I hear no such thing, and finally Elizabeth sets her knife and fork down once her plate is empty.

"Will there be pudding?" she asks.

"I... Yes," I stammer, "I mean... I can heat up some of yesterday's apple pie."

"I'm not really very hungry," she replies,

looking rather nervous. “Might I be excused to go to my room and do some homework? We have a big test coming up, all about our times tables. I suppose I should do well if I want to attract a good husband some day.”

“Of course, darling,” I tell her.

She immediately gets to her feet and hurries to the sink, where she deposits her plate and cutlery before heading to the door.

“I shall come back to wash up shortly,” she explains. “Thank you, Mother.”

“It's quite alright,” I reply. “But Elizabeth, if -”

Before I can finish, I hear her hurry up the stairs. I take a deep breath, telling myself that I could have handled that situation better, and then I glance into the hallway and see Elizabeth's school bag resting next to her shoes.

I hesitate for a moment, and then I get to my feet and make my way over to the bag. I know there is nothing untoward going on here, but it would be as well to prove to myself that the voice was wrong. I glance up the stairs to make sure that Elizabeth is not about to come down, and then I kneel and unbuckle the bag. All I shall find inside, I am sure, is Elizabeth's school books and pencils, and I must admit that I feel rather wicked right now. A mother should not doubt her daughter,

And then I spot the rose.

Nestled in the bag, tucked to the side of the books, there rests a single red rose. The head is slightly crushed, presumably due to being bumped by the books, but as I carefully slip the rose out I see that it is of a very rich red color, with large, sharp thorns on the stem.

"She met an older man in the forest," the voice whispers. "He wants to do things to her, the same things an older man once did to you. The poor girl hasn't quite given in just yet, but she will. And who can blame her? Anything's better than going to school and being bullied by those three nasty girls."

I pause, before shaking my head.

"You think she picked it herself?" the voice asks. "And put it in her own bag? That's possible, I suppose. Some girls might do that. But not Elizabeth. She is desperately unhappy, Judith. Most days, instead of going to school, she wanders alone in the forest. It was inevitable that eventually she'd bump into someone."

"No," I say firmly.

"He meets her often, he offers her flattery and roses."

"You're lying!"

"What kind of decent man just hangs around in the forest and strikes up conversations with young girls that he meets. He's from a nearby farm. Elizabeth's just a young girl, Judith. He flatters her and he makes her feel as if she's more mature than her years. You know that sort of thing will work on her eventually. He's just opening her plump, naive little heart millimeter by millimeter with each touch. With each kiss. With each gesture. And then he's going to walk straight inside and do and take whatever he wants. By the time he's done, she'll still be thanking him. By the time she realizes what a mistake she's made, she'll already have been ruined."

With tears in my eyes, I shake my head again.

"After all," the voice says, "it once worked on you."

"That was different."

"Life is hard for a single mother. People talk, Judith. You know that better than anyone else in Briarwych."

"No," I say firmly, as I slide the rose back into place. My hands are trembling, and at the last moment I prick one finger on a thorn. I wince, but a drop of blood has already fallen onto one of Elizabeth's school books.

"Nothing has happened yet," the voice says. "She has not suffered that moment of weakness that you once suffered. Oh, I know you are glad to have Elizabeth, but you can never quite wipe away the shame, can you? Two times you have been sorely tempted. The first time, with the rock and Prudence Williams, you just about held back. The second time, with that man, you gave in. Do you want Elizabeth to make the same mistake?"

"She wouldn't," I whisper.

"She might. After all, she seems to take after you very much."

"She has a wise head on her shoulders," I say as I close the bag. "She knows not to do such things."

"Keep telling yourself that, Judith. Meanwhile, she will leave the house tomorrow morning, claiming she is going to school. But how do you know that tomorrow won't be the day when she makes her terrible mistake? Think how the locals would gossip, Judith, if the daughter followed the mother and ended up with a big, round belly?"

"This isn't real," I say as I get to my feet. "You're not real."

"I was right about Violet Durridge, wasn't I?" she asks. "Do you want the details of what I did to that woman, Judith? Do you want to know how she fell asleep in her bed, with a cigarette in her hand? Do you want to know how I slowly moved her hand down to the bed-sheets, and how I then held the woman down as the flames roared? I thought you'd be happy this evening. After all, you seem to like the local priest a great deal."

"No!" I gasp, before turning and hurrying back into the kitchen, where I go straight to the sink and start doing the washing. If I just keep working, I shall have no time to imagine these voices.

"I can help you, Judith," the voice says. "I would *like* to help you."

I start banging the pots as I wash, hoping to drown the voice out so that hopefully it will then cease entirely.

"Oh Judith," the voice sighs, "let me prove myself to you again. Elizabeth is not going to school tomorrow. She will claim that she is, and then she will go to meet her new friend at Cobbler's Bottom in the forest. If I'm wrong, or if I'm not real, then what harm is there in going there at about midday and seeing for yourself?"

"No," I say through gritted teeth, banging the pots more loudly. "No, I shall not."

The voice says something else, but I bump the saucepan several times against the side of the sink, drowning out the words. At first this does not work, and then after maybe half a minute I realize that the voice seems to have gone. I keep bumping the saucepan, however, as I wait in case the voice returns. If I hear that wretched thing again, I think I might very well explode with rage.

"Mother?"

Letting out a startled shriek, I turn and see that Elizabeth is standing in the doorway.

"Are you alright?" she asks. "I could hear you making such a noise down here."

"I'm fine," I say, although I am a little

breathless. "Are you ready for school tomorrow?"

"I shall be," she replies, "after I have done a little more reading. I was going to ask, is it okay if I don't help with the washing this evening? I have so much to read and I'm worried it won't all sink in if it's rushed."

"Of course," I reply, and I watch as she goes over and picks up her school bag. "And you *are* going to school tomorrow, aren't you?"

"Yes, Mother," she says, already heading up the stairs, "of course. Where else would I go?"

CHAPTER SIX

I WATCH FROM THE kitchen window as Elizabeth carries her school bag out into the lane, and then I watch as she walks away. It should take her about an hour to reach the school, and she certainly looks as if that's where she's going. She's wearing her uniform, and her bag looks heavy with books.

Of course she's going to school. I would never dream of thinking otherwise.

***

The clock strikes eleven as I continue to sweep dust from the floor. My knees rest uncomfortably on the church's cold stone, at the base of the steps that lead up to the altar, but this morning I am not troubled by such things. Indeed, all morning I have been noticing the time, as nine o'clock gave way to ten, and then to eleven. Now there is just one hour to go before noon, and I am struggling to remain calm.

"Elizabeth is not going to school tomorrow," the voice told me last night. "She will claim that she is, and then she will go to meet her new friend at Cobbler's Bottom in the forest. If I'm wrong, or if I'm not real, then what harm is there in going there at about midday and seeing for yourself?"

It's all nonsense, of course. I know that, deep down. Yet the words linger in my mind, almost taunting me, and I feel that by midday I shall be in a terrible state. I keep imagining Elizabeth out there in the forest, alone or perhaps even with a man. I was once in a very similar situation myself, and I allowed myself a momentary slip.

Finally, getting to my feet, I head through to the corridor and then I stop in the doorway and watch for a moment as Father Perkins continues with his work. He seems so calm, so peaceful, that I hesitate to disturb him. At the same time, he is the only person who can possibly help me right now.

"Might I ask you something?" I say after a few seconds.

"Hmm?" He continues to write. "What is it, Judith?"

"I wanted to ask you about voices," I

continue. "A friend of mine, more of an acquaintance, has a sister who has heard voices. Rather, she has heard one voice, only a few times. But the voice tells her things. This friend wants some advice on what might bc happening, and I was wondering what you thought?"

"Hearing voices?" He turns to me. "I'm afraid to say that voices might be a sign of madness."

I take a deep breath.

"I knew of a woman in Lancaster Gate once," he continues, "who claimed to hear voices. It was a frightful matter for all concerned, especially for her poor family. On and on it all went, and she didn't respond to any treatments. Do you know what happened to the poor woman, Judith?"

"What?"

"She threw herself out of the window. She might have survived, but unfortunately she landed right in the path of a vehicle and, well, that was the end of that. Right before she jumped, she claimed that the voices were telling her she could fly. Can you imagine that? I think she genuinely believed she might flap her arms and fly up into the sky like a bird." He sniffs. "Madness makes its mark in so many different ways."

"Alright," I say cautiously, "but what if the voices are telling her very *specific* things?"

"Such as that she can fly?"

“More serious things,” I continue, trying not to let my impatience become apparent. “About the world around her.”

“I'm not sure that I follow you, Judith.”

“Secrets. Things that nobody should know, but which subsequently turn out to have been true.”

“That seems highly improbable.”

“Of course,” I say, forcing a smile in an attempt to seem unconcerned. “Yet this is what my friend's niece claims. And it seems that there is some corroborating evidence.”

“Niece? I thought you said it was her sister?”

“Of course. Her sister. Her niece's mother.” I try again to smile, but I am afraid I am not doing a good job. “Is it possible that the Lord is speaking directly to her?”

“The Lord?”

“And maybe in a female voice?”

“I'm not sure what you mean,” he replies. “Judith, it sounds to me as if your friend should be assessed by a doctor. Either that, or perhaps there is some kind of demonic activity.”

He turns back to his papers.

“Demonic?” I ask cautiously.

“It's said that demons come to test us from time to time,” he says as he starts writing again. “I'm not sure I believe that such things happen in quite such a direct fashion. Your friend's sister should be seen by someone, though. It's best to nip these things in the bud."

"Of course, Father," I say as I step back out into the corridor. "Thank you."

Stopping and leaning against the wall, I try to get my thoughts together. I know that I am not mad, and I am certain that the voice I heard was not a demon. That leaves only one possibility, which is that perhaps the Lord is trying to warn me about something. The whole business with Violet Durridge was a misunderstanding that I cannot quite sort out, but perhaps the Lord is trying to warn me about Elizabeth. In that case, it is my duty as a mother to go out to Cobbler's Bottom and see for myself.

***

The leaves rustle beneath my feet as I make my way through the forest. I should have brought a coat but I did not, so I am shivering slightly as I hurry between the trees. All around me, fallen leaves are rotting slightly on the ground, and there is no possibility of sneaking through the forest today. My approach will surely be heard, yet – as I get closer and closer to the dip that leads down to Cobbler's Bottom – I am more certain than ever that I shall find nothing out here. Elizabeth is at this moment sitting at her desk at school, and I am about to prove to myself that the voice is just an aberration.

And then, stopping suddenly, I see a man walking along in the distance.

He is quite alone, and when I squint I am just about able to see that he is a handsome, rather strapping young man who looks to be in his twenties. I can just about make out stubble on his chin, but he walks without a limp and my first thought is that this man should be fighting for his country instead of traipsing through the forest. He might work on a farm, as the voice suggested; then again, perhaps he works at the nearby RAF base. I watch as he wanders along, and I wait until he is out of sight. Evidently he did not hear or notice me. He is heading roughly in the direction of the airbase, so I tell myself that he is merely an airman who happened to come out here when he had a spare moment. That makes sense.

I wait a moment longer, and then I resume my walk toward Cobbler's Bottom. My heart is racing, and I feel a faint fear tugging at my heart, no matter how many times I tell myself that there is no reason to be concerned.

In my mind's eye, I imagine Elizabeth sitting studiously at her desk, raising her hand to answer all the questions that the teacher asks. She is such a bright girl, and resilient to boot. I imagine that all the other girls are simply jealous of her prodigious gifts. Often, the most intelligent girls are the ones who are scorned by their classmates. Nevertheless, I am sure that Elizabeth will carry on with her work. It is simply inconceivable that she would stray from the proper path.

Suddenly I stop in my tracks as I see a figure in the distance.

It's her.

I know immediately, from the dress and from the way that she's walking. I recognize my dear Elizabeth, and I see that she is walking away from Cobbler's Bottom, heading in the opposite direction to the man I saw a moment earlier. I feel the most dreadful sense of despair in my chest as I realize that I was wrong to have so much faith in her, that she is not at school at all. And as she walks, she is holding something in her hands, and I squint just in time to see that she is sniffing another long-stemmed rose.

I think my heart is breaking.

She has not seen me, despite the noise of my feet against the leaves. I suppose her feet make an equal noise. And as she wanders away, she seems to be in something of a daze. I think I can see that she is smiling, and somehow deep down I already know that she must have been meeting that man. I open my mouth to call out, but no words emerge and I suddenly realize that my knees feel weak. I try to steady myself, but then I have to go and lean against the nearest tree, lest I might collapse entirely. The whole world seems to be swinging all around me, and I swear I can feel an actual pain in my chest where my heart is suffering.

"Oh Elizabeth," I whimper, with tears running down my face, "why did you have to do this? Didn't I warn you? Didn't I tell you that it was wrong? Why didn't you learn from my example?"

In all my life, I have never felt so low. I have made mistakes of my own, of course, but for the first time I am seeing that my own daughter is following in my footsteps. I have failed her as a mother, and – worse – I have been blind to the truth. I have been vain and conceited and gullible. I have been a fool.

"You are no fool, Judith," the voice says suddenly. "Have I done enough now? Do you understand that I am real?"

"Who are you?" I ask, as my bottom lip trembles. "What do you want?"

"I already told you," the voice replies. "I want to help you. And I want you to stop doubting yourself so much. Elizabeth has her own mind. Yes, she is your daughter, but she makes her own decisions. And whereas you had no such warnings as a girl, she has had many. She has ignored your advice."

"She's a good girl," I stammer.

"Then save her," the voice says. "If she is worth saving, you must do it. Do not hide away from the truth, Judith. Confront it. Rage at it, if you must. But if you truly believe that your girl is good, it would be a sin not to go right now and save her from her own mistakes."

I hesitate for a moment, before nodding.

"Then go to it," the voice adds. "I shall help. We can do it together."

Stepping away from the tree, I start walking once again through the forest, heading after Elizabeth. I pick up my pace, almost running as I hurry between the trees. Elizabeth has a considerable head-start, but in my mind's eye I can only think about catching up to her and confronting her. My anger is building, getting stronger and stronger until it throbs in my chest, and I know I am going to have to be tough with my darling girl. Perhaps I have been too gentle with her in the past, but that approach has clearly not worked and this time I fear I must be stern. And as I walk even faster than before, crunching across the bed of leaves, I clench my fists.

After a few more minutes I spot her in the distance. She is still wandering along slowly, admiring the rose, but then she turns and looks this way. I see the look of horror and fear in her eyes as soon as she realizes she has been caught, and she hesitates for a few seconds before turning and running.

"Elizabeth Prendergast!" I shout at the top

of my voice. “Come here!”

Still she runs, so I too start running, setting off after her and getting faster and faster until I am racing between the trees. I do not remember the last time I actually ran, and I am surprised by my speed. Perhaps it is my anger that is driving me onward, but I realize rather quickly that I am catching Elizabeth. It is as if some deeper strength is filling my body, and now I am only a few paces behind her. I am getting breathless, but – as I reach out toward Elizabeth's back – I am determined to stop her and make her understand.

“Get back here!” I shout. “You can't run forever!”

She lets out a faint gasp as she tries to go faster.

“I said get back here!” I scream. “Elizabeth!”

With that, I manage to grab her by the shoulder, and I pull her down as I slam into her and send her crashing down against the forest floor. Landing on top of her, I stare down into her terrified eyes and then I scream again.

CHAPTER SEVEN

OPENING MY EYES, I see the cold, dark stone floor of the church, and my own hands clenched together in prayer. I stay completely still for a moment, listening to the silence, and then I raise my face and see that altar of Briarwych Church at the top of the steps. I am freezing cold, and the church is lit only by streams of moonlight that bathe everything in a pale blue color. I am on my knees before the altar, in the position of prayer.

I do not remember how I got here.

For a moment, I do not remember much at all, but then I realize that I was chasing Elizabeth through the forest. I was running faster and faster, desperately trying to catch up to her. I was filled with anger, and finally I grabbed her from behind. I pulled her down and landed on her, and then I put my hands on her throat to hold her down. She was kicking and fighting furiously, but I screamed at her and then...

And then what?

It was daytime when I caught her in the forest, only a little after noon. Now it is dark outside and many, many hours must have passed. Evidently I returned to Briarwych, but I remember none of that. It is as if the past few hours have been wiped from my mind, and I have absolutely no idea what happened in the forest or what I did or where Elizabeth is now.

Slowly, I get to my feet. My knees are trembling slightly and I have to support myself against one of the pews. Looking around, I realize that I am all alone. I head along the aisle and through to the corridor, and then I check the various rooms to see whether Father Perkins is here. He is not, which is unusual, and I am still rather worried by the fact that I seem to have no memory whatsoever of my return to the village.

What happened out there in the forest?

***

As soon as I push the front door open, I feel a rush of relief as I hear Elizabeth working in the kitchen. The lights are on and the house is warm, and Elizabeth seems to be doing her chores. Perhaps everything is right again.

I head over to the kitchen door and look through, and I am surprised to see Elizabeth down on her hands and knees, scrubbing the floor. Indeed, the entire kitchen is immaculate, and I turn and see that the whole house seems to have been cleaned from top to bottom. I clean regularly, of course, but this is of another magnitude. I honestly do not remember the last time the house looked so good.

I turn back to look at Elizabeth.

"My darling," I say, "I -"

She lets out a startled cry and spins around, backing against the cupboard door and staring at me with wild, fearful eyes. It is as if she had not heard me enter the house.

"My darling," I continue cautiously, "what a pleasant surprise. You have done such a wonderful job."

I wait, but if anything the fear in her eyes seems to have grown. She looks positively terrified.

"I never knew you were so good at cleaning," I say with a smile, before stepping into the room. "Why, even the stove -"

Before I have managed a single pace, Elizabeth scrambles back across the floor and then stops in the far corner, as if she wants to keep as far away from me as possible. For a moment, I cannot quite believe what is happening. Elizabeth and I have had our disagreements in the past, of course, but she has never acted like this before.

"Whatever is the matter?" I ask, still smiling. "You seem to be in rather a state."

Her lips tremble, and I think she is trying to say something. She is staring at me with such terror, however, that I finally turn and look over my shoulder, just in case something dreadful is behind me, and then I turn to her again.

"Elizabeth," I continue, "whatever is the matter? You are beginning to worry me."

"I did it," she stammers, her voice trembling so much that she can barely get the words out. "I'll do more, I swear. I won't sleep. I'll work all night."

"That seems rather unnecessary," I point out. "My darling, why are you shaking so badly? Everything is fine." I pause, before making my way around the kitchen table, and this time Elizabeth merely shrinks a little further into the corner. I stop and reach a hand out toward her. "You have done more than enough for one night. Are you hungry?"

As I ask that question, I realize that I too am hungry. Ravenous, even. Is it possible that Elizabeth and I have not had dinner tonight? I always have food on the table for six o'clock, yet there is no sign of anything having been prepared. I do not want to admit to Elizabeth that I have forgotten the events of the past few hours, but at the same time I know that I must feed my daughter.

"I can make something quick and simple," I

say, with my hand still outstretched. "Come on, get up off the floor and have a wash. By the time you're done, I shall have something on the table. Perhaps I shall make one of your favorites."

She lets out a faint, pained murmur.

"Elizabeth, please," I continue, "you must get up now."

She hesitates, and then – ignoring my hand – she slowly hauls herself up. She seems a little stiff, as if she's in some discomfort, and she's still staring at me with that same expression of abject horror.

"Are you okay?" I ask cautiously. "Elizabeth, are you hurt?"

She shakes her head.

"Are you sure?" I continue. "Elizabeth, are you -"

"I'm fine!" she blurts out. "Please don't ask! I told you I'm fine, and I'm not lying! Not this time! Not everything I tell you is a lie!" She pauses, and now she seems a little breathless. "I *can* tell the truth, you know," she adds. "Sometimes."

"My darling, I know," I say, stepping toward her, "I merely -"

She pulls away and hurries around the table, stopping next to the doorway.

"Whyever are you frightened?" I ask, although I'm already terrified that I must have said or done something terrible in the forest. I hope I did not strike her in a moment of anger, but – again – I do not want to ask her directly. “My darling,” I continue, “I had to admonish you, but the moment has passed now and we should not let any negative feelings fester. Come on, let's have something to eat.”

“Can I be excused and go to my room?”

“Have you eaten?”

“I don't want to eat,” she whimpers, as tears fill her eyes. “I'm not hungry. I just want to go to bed and sleep.”

“Are you feeling ill?”

She shakes her head, as her bottom lip trembles and tears start running down her cheeks.

“My darling,” I say, once again stepping toward her, “whatever is the -”

“Just let me go to bed!” she shouts, pulling back and bumping hard against the jamb of the door. She seems to be limping a little. “I'll be fine in the morning! I just need to sleep now! Why won't you let me sleep?”

“Of course you can sleep,” I tell her, as I realize that she is perhaps just letting her hormones run riot. After all, she is a young girl, and her feelings might be a little raw. “We can talk in the morning.”

“I don't want to go to school tomorrow,” she says through gritted teeth.

“My dear, I think it would be good if -”

"I don't want to go to school tomorrow!" she snaps angrily.

"Fine," I reply, hoping to avert an argument. "You can have a little time off, and then the weekend will give you a chance for a fuller rest. Does that sound acceptable?"

"I'll be okay," she stammers, before turning and running up the stairs, and then slamming her bedroom door shut.

"She's just embarrassed," I whisper, as I step back against the counter and try to make sense of this madness. "There's nothing more to it. She's embarrassed, and she'll be fine. This time tomorrow, everything will be alright again."

As I say those words, however, I already know that tomorrow morning I must get to the bottom of this all. Starting with the voice that I keep hearing in the church.

CHAPTER EIGHT

LOITERING CLOSE TO THE noticeboard, I watch as Father Perkins finally emerges from the church. I've been here for hours, determined to watch him leave but also not wanting to speak to him until I understand what is happening. He gets onto his bicycle and starts to cycle away, and I feel a growing sense of fear as he disappears from view.

I must not be weak.

I slip into the cemetery and make my way along the path. With each step that takes me closer to the church, I feel the sense of fear getting stronger, but I force myself to keep going. By the time I reach the door, my hands are trembling, but I step into the church and then I immediately walk along the aisle until I'm at the foot of the altar, and there I kneel. Instead of lowering my face in prayer, however, I stare up at the altar and listen for a moment to the silence of the church.

"Okay," I say finally, unable to rid my voice of fear, "I accept that you are real. Now tell me what you really are."

***

"So you're not the Lord?" I ask, sitting on the steps and looking back along the aisle. "I thought..."

My voice trails off.

"You thought your prayers were finally going to be answered, after so long?" the voice asks. "That's cute."

"Then I still don't understand," I continue. "Are you an angel?"

I hear a faint ripple of laughter.

"Are you..."

For a moment, I cannot bring myself to say the word.

"Are you a demon?" I ask finally.

The laughter stops.

"You humans have such silly words for these things," the voice says eventually. "These words are alien to me. I do not know what an angel is, or a demon."

I take a deep breath. Is this some kind of trick?

"I am an intelligence," the voice continues,

"that for many centuries had been drifting around. I could have attached myself to any passing human soul, but nothing caught my fancy. And I *do* still have standards. So I waited and waited, and to be honest I was starting to lose interest in the whole thing. Then, one hot day, I saw two young girls walking through the forest and making their way out to a field. I almost didn't pay any attention, for I have found young human girls to be so dull in the past, but for some reason I decided to come to the edge of the forest and watch for a while."

"What does this have to do with me?" I ask.

"Do you not remember?" the voice replies. "I think you do. It was so hot, your friend partially disrobed."

I feel a shudder pass through my body.

"And then *you*, Judith, took a rock and -"

"No!" I blurt out, getting to my feet and taking a few steps backward. "That did not happen!"

"But it nearly did," the voice explains, "and for a moment, just a moment, you thought that you'd bashed your friend's skull open. I found the whole scene fascinating, Judith. I have seen humans getting overcome by their desires before, but you fought back, you managed to control yourself. And I continued to watch the pair of you with great interest. That was the moment when I realized that I had finally chanced upon a soul that was worthy of my time. I have been watching ever since, keeping an eye on things, waiting for certain souls to mature."

"You're lying," I stammer, backing away again until I bump against one of the pews. "That was years ago!"

"You try so hard to keep your dark side hidden, Judith. You smother your darkness in hypocrisy and fear. You've built a cage out of your faith, and you're scared to stray beyond those bars. You did stray one more time, though, didn't you? With the man whose seed grew in your belly. I was glad when that happened, Judith. It showed me that the struggle was still very real in your heart."

I shake my head.

"You took a crucifix from your friend that day," the voice says.

"She gave it to me."

"And what happened to it?"

"I lost it," I explain. "I wish I hadn't, but one day it was gone."

"Really?"

Suddenly something falls in front of me, and I hear a faint bumping sound as I look down and see that the crucifix is now at my feet. Reaching down, I pick it up, convinced that it must turn out to be a facsimile. Somehow, as soon as I feel the crucifix in my hand I know that it is the same one that I lost all those years ago.

"You were careless and dropped it," the voice says. "I saved it for when you would want to see it again."

"And how did you feel when you learned of Violet's violent end?" she asks. "Be honest. How did you really feel?"

"Shocked," I tell her. "Horrified.

"Don't lie."

"I thought it was quite awful."

"Don't lie, Judith."

"I...

I pause for a moment.

"Happy," I say finally, and then I close my eyes as I realize that I am still, after all these years, a terrible person. "I hated her. I judged her. She got in my way and I am still glad that she died. I hated her for -"

Suddenly I let out a gasp as I realize how awful I have become. Opening my eyes, I know now that the Lord must have known this about me all along. I am not, and can never be, a good person.

"I'm glad that you have finally stopped lying," the voice says. "After all, I do not lie to you, so why should you lie to me? And what about yesterday? Are you happy that I intervened to show you what Elizabeth was really doing?"

"I had to stop her," I reply, "but..."

I think back to the moment when I fell upon Elizabeth and screamed at her.

"I do not remember what happened," I admit finally. "I was in the forest and then I was here in the church, and now Elizabeth looks at me as if I am some kind of monster."

"You disciplined her."

"How?"

"She will not see that man again."

"But what did I say to her?" I ask. "What did I do?"

I wait for an answer.

"Were you there?" I add finally. "Do you know what happened?"

"I was there," the voice replies. "I was so proud of you."

"What did I do?" I shout.

"You are her mother, Judith. You set her back onto the straight path, and this time she will not stray again. In years to come, she will thank you for everything."

"Why don't I remember?" I whisper, with tears in my eyes.

"You don't *need* to remember. The task is complete, and that is what matters. If you really *must* remember the afternoon in the forest, the answer can be found wrapped in linen in the bottom drawer of your chest. The one in your bedroom. You put this answer there yourself. But do not torment yourself, Judith. I think it would upset you to know the truth. Simply be glad that the girl has learned her lesson."

"I don't want you going anywhere near my daughter," I say firmly.

"You should be pleased with how things have developed," she replies. "There is so much more that I can do. Why don't we have a little discussion about certain matters?"

"I'm not going to listen to this," I reply, as I turn and start walking away. "I don't know what you are, but this is wrong and I refuse to -"

"Shaltak."

I stop in my tracks, but I am too scared to turn around. I do not know why, but I am suddenly filled with the most terrible sense of dread. It is as if that name – which I have never heard before in my life – nevertheless flickers in my soul with some deep, long-lost meaning.

"My name," she continues, "is Shaltak. Does that name fill you with horror, Judith Prendergast? I doubt very much that you have heard it before, but perhaps some echo lives on in all human minds. After all, I was once very famous, back in the very old days."

"I don't know who you are," I say through gritted teeth, although at the same time I have to wonder why the name Shaltak fills me with such dread.

"I think the name reverberates in your soul," she says. "My name reverberates in all human souls.

You have no idea how much pleasure this confirmation gives me. Now come and sit with me."

"I would rather die," I say, before making my way along the aisle.

"You'll change your mind," her voice purrs. "You'll come crawling back to me, begging for my help."

"I shall not," I whisper under my breath as I head outside. "There is nothing you can offer me that would make me turn to you."

CHAPTER NINE

"IT WAS WORTH A try," Father Perkins says the next day, as we sit sipping tea in his office, "but evidently Violet truly had no family at all. So the funeral will take place on Monday, and I suppose it shall be a rather forlorn affair."

"Indeed," I reply. "It is saddening to think that somebody could be all alone in the world like that."

"It can be difficult to find one's way," he says with a nod. "I myself sometimes find myself thinking that I should be out there fighting."

"No!" I say firmly. "You are needed here in Briarwych!"

"There's a war raging, Judith," he says with a sigh. "Yes, I am needed here, but perhaps I am needed *more* out there. Young men are getting wounded, and are seeing their friends dying. They're killing other young men. Sometimes I wonder whether the Lord would make better use of me in the theater of war. And if I believe in the cause, I mean if I *truly* believe in it, should I not fight? I'm too old to be called up, but they would take me if I forced the matter, I'm sure."

"I rather think that you underestimate the importance of your role here," I tell him. "The war won't last forever. It's important that those young men, when they eventually return, find that their home is waiting here for them. We have to keep England ticking over until then."

I take a sip of tea, before glancing at Father Perkins and seeing that he is staring at me with a faint, quizzical smile on his face. He appears rather bemused.

"What's wrong?" I ask, worried that perhaps I have spilled or committed some kind of faux pas.

"Nothing," he says, "just..."

His voice trails off for a moment.

"You look different today, Judith," he adds finally. "More... I don't know the exact word, but you look more alive. More radiant, I suppose. You're almost glowing."

"I don't see why that should be," I tell him. "I am simply myself."

"It's quite remarkable," he replies.

"I'm sorry."

"No, don't be." He stares at me for a few more seconds. "Have you done your hair differently?"

"I have not."

"Your make-up, then?"

"I wear none."

"Your clothes, then." Suddenly he gets to his feet and takes a few steps toward me. "Stand up, Judith. Please."

I hesitate, and then I get to my feet.

"There is something different about you," he continues. "I know I am hardly the most observant man in the world, but I am absolutely certain that there has been some great change in your countenance. Whatever might it be, Judith?"

"I do not know," I say, as I set my cup down and take a step back, "but I'm afraid I must attend to some matters in the -"

"No, stay!" he blurts out. "Please. At least for one more cup of tea."

I open my mouth to decline the offer, but then I realize that this might be the first time Father Perkins has *ever* been so keen for my company. I should go back to my duties, yet somehow I feel that I cannot.

"One more," I say, and he is already taking my cup back over to get a refill. "But then I really must do some work. One cannot sit and drink tea all day long."

"How is Elizabeth doing?" he asks.

"She is fine," I reply, bristling slightly. "Why do you ask?"

"Just making conversation," he says. "She's such a lovely girl. She's a real testament to you, you know. You should be proud."

"That's very kind of you."

"I know it can't have been easy, raising her alone." He brings my cup over and sets it next to me. "I want you to know, Judith, that I have nothing but the utmost respect for you. I understand the circumstances around Elizabeth's arrival were somewhat trying, and that perhaps you have attracted some opprobrium on account of the fact that you were not married. I just want you to know that I have always considered you to be above reproach, Judith. In fact, in some ways I have admired you a great deal."

"I don't know what to say," I reply, as I feel myself starting to blush. "I have always done my best, but that hardly marks me out as anything special."

"It does, Judith," he replies, and then he stares at me for a moment. "Any man would be lucky to have you as his wife."

We stand in silence for a few seconds. I most certainly do not know how to respond to everything Father Perkins has just said, and I most certainly believe that he is being over-generous. As the seconds drag on, however, I begin to wonder whether it would be wise for me to make an excuse and leave.

"I really should get back to work," I tell him finally.

"Of course," he replies, "but promise me that we shall talk again soon. Like this."

"I should be honored," I say, before turning and heading out of the room, leaving my second cup of tea untouched. Glancing back, I see that Father Perkins is watching me leave, and I smile briefly at him before making my way along the corridor.

By the time I get to the front door, I am trembling with nerves. If I did not know better, I would be tempted to believe that Father Perkins intends to propose to me.

***

Stepping out of the church, I make my way around the side of the building, hoping to find a quiet spot where I can regain my composure. Since leaving Father Perkins' office I have been replaying his words over and over again, and it is quite clear that his attitude to me has changed drastically.

I have long hoped that he would see me as a potential wife, but I had perhaps grown accustomed to the thought that this would never happen. Now he seems rather keen, and I cannot help but think that he would make a wonderful, respectable husband. He would surely be a fine step-father for Elizabeth too. And since I have never actually been married, there would seem to be no stumbling blocks other than the disapproval of a few local figures.

My heart is racing as I lean back against the wall and take a deep breath.

The voice has been silent today, which I take as a sign that it was perhaps never real in the first place. How it made such accurate prediction, I shall never know, but perhaps it was merely saying things that I knew deep down to be true. I had a moment of madness, but that moment has now passed and calm has returned to my life. I was going to ask Father Perkins about the voice again, although now I fear that course of action might only make matters worse. So long as I do not hear the voice again, everything will be fine.

Suddenly spotting movement in the distance, I turn and look over toward the gate, and I am surprised to see that Elizabeth is halfway along the path. She is looking toward the church's main door, and she seems not to have noticed me at all. Instead, she looks rather nervous, as if she wants to go into the church but is too afraid. A moment later she takes a step forward, then she stops again, and then she half-turns as if she is too scared to go any further. Finally, she turns and starts to walk away, still limping slightly.

"Elizabeth!" I call out.

She stops and turns to me.

"Is anything the matter?" I ask as I head over to her. I am making a very special effort to smile, to put her at ease. I want to get rid of the fear that's in her eyes.

She hesitates, and for a moment I worry that she might be about to turn and run. Then, as if she has summoned some extra courage, she waits for me to get closer.

"I have been speaking to Father Perkins," I explain. "He's really a very nice gentleman, Elizabeth. Perhaps you would like to get to know him a little better? If you have any worries, he is always available for a discrete word or two."

"It's fine," she replies, barely able to meet my gaze. "I'm sorry if I'm disturbing you, it's just..."

She pauses again.

"It's just what, darling?"

"There's a lady here to see you," she continues. "She's at home. I didn't know how long you'd be, so I told her I'd come and see if you're free."

"A lady?" I try to think who this could be. Everybody knows that I spend my days at the church, so an inhabitant of the village would simply come here if they needed something. And I do not know many people from beyond Briarwych. "What is her name?"

"I didn't catch a name," she says, "but she asked for you specifically. I think it's quite urgent."

"This is a rather inconvenient time, Elizabeth. Can't you ask her to come back later?"

"I *did* suggest that, but she was most insistent."

"Fine," I mutter, even though I would much rather get on with my work. "I suppose I can spare a few minutes to pop home and see what this is all about."

I step past Elizabeth but then, realizing that she doesn't seem to be coming with me, I glance back toward her.

"Are you coming?"

"Of course," she says, and then she starts obediently coming this way.

Supposing that she is still in a strange mood after whatever happened in the forest, I start walking out of the cemetery. I desperately want to talk some more to Elizabeth, to ask what she's thinking, but I'm wary of pushing too much. She will talk to me when she's ready, and I'm sure she's just feeling embarrassed about the fact that I caught her lying yesterday. She'll come around soon enough.

Reaching the cottage, I stop for a moment and check that I am presentable, and then I turn to see that Elizabeth is dawdling quite a way behind me. It's almost as if she is scared of getting too close.

"Are you coming in?" I ask her.

"You wanted me to fetch some things from the shop," she replies cautiously.

"Then don't take too long," I continue. "You might be away from school today, but you are most certainly not a lady of leisure."

I smile, but she does not reciprocate. Instead, she hesitates for a moment before turning and hurrying back along the lane. I swear, that girl seems to be in a terrible state at the moment. Sighing, I open the cottage's front door and make my way through to the living room, where I find that here is a lady waiting for me.

"Good morning," I say, as the lady sets down her cup of tea and turns to me, "I'm sorry for -"

Stopping suddenly, I see the lady's face and feel a shudder of recognition.

"Judith, how are you?" Prudence Williams says as she gets to her feet. "I wonder, do you remember me?"

CHAPTER TEN

"I'VE BEEN ALL OVER the place, really," Prue explains as we sit with fresh cups of tea. "After my parents left Briarwych, I ended up in Macclesfield for a while, then Congleton. The war rather put the kibosh on Daddy's plans and, well, we've been rather rootless. And then, not too long ago, I started thinking about lovely little Briarwych, and I decided to come back for a visit."

"How pleasant," I say, trying to pretend that I am pleased to see her.

"Not much has changed, has it?" she adds. "Sometimes I think sweet little Briarwych will just sit here forever, ignoring the forces of the outside world. Why, if you told me that fifty or a hundred years from now the place would be much the same, I'd have no trouble whatsoever believing you. Now

London, that's a place that keeps leaping on all the time, even with all this wretched misery going on at the moment. I say, Judith, do you think there might be a -"

"Is there something in particular that you wanted?" I ask, cutting her off. I immediately realize that I have perhaps been a little short with her, so I take a deep breath and try to recover my composure. "I'm sorry," I continue, "it's just that I have many duties to consider at the church. I'm sure you'll understand."

"Conscientious as ever, eh?"

"One does one's best."

She pauses, eyeing me with a hint of concern.

"Actually, it wasn't just Briarwych that popped back into my mind," she continues. "I've been thinking a lot about you too, Judith."

"Me?" I force a smile. "I can't imagine why."

"Well, we were friends. That's one reason."

I look over at the window for a moment. I don't know why, but Prue's sudden reappearance after all these years has left me feeling distinctly uncomfortable. We weren't exactly good friends, we were merely girls of roughly the same age who naturally spent some time together. When she and her family left Briarwych, I wasn't even particularly troubled, and I certainly never expected to see her again. I should not really care too much one way or the other, but I rather feel as if my skin is beginning to crawl.

"Do you remember that very hot day?" she asks suddenly.

I turn to her again.

"You and I went for a walk," she continues, "and we ended up in one of the fields out of town. The whole day was hot, but for a few minutes the heat just seemed to become absolutely unbearable. It was as if the fires of Hell briefly reached up and tried to cook us alive. Oh do tell me that you remember, Judith."

"I think so," I reply, slightly surprised that she's bringing that day up so quickly. After all, I was reminded of it by that awful voice just a short while ago. "Why do you ask?"

"I don't know, really," she says, "but it's been on my mind of late. I know this is going to sound awfully strange, Judith, but I feel as if something changed on that day. It was just a day or two later that Mummy and Daddy told me that we were to move away, and I suppose that's when I began to feel less like a little girl and more like a grown woman. Everyone probably has a story like that, but... Well, I've been thinking about it a lot lately."

She pauses, as if she expects me to say something, but I honestly don't know what she really wants.

"I haven't felt the same since that day," she adds. "Have you, Judith?"

"It's difficult to remember," I tell her.

"You didn't notice a sudden change?"

"Not that I recall."

"And now?" She pauses. "I'm sorry, Judith, but I just feel as if we endured something together on that day, all those years ago. Am I just imagining things?"

"I'm sure that everything is alright," I reply. "There's really no need to fuss over trivial matters."

"Anyway, I was close to Briarwych," she continues, sounding a little nervous, "and I had a few days to kill, and I thought of you and I decided to come and drop in to see you. You're the only person I really remember with any fondness from the old days, Judith. Oh, tell me I'm not making a fool of myself. I'm terribly worried now that you're about to say that you barely remember me."

"Of course I remember you," I tell her, not for the first time since I came into the room. "And I remember that day, too."

"It was stiflingly hot."

"It was."

"I had to take off my dress."

"Did you?" I think back to that moment. "Yes. Yes, you did."

"And I fell asleep for a few minutes."

I swallow hard.

"Yes," I say, "you did."

"Did you fall asleep too?"

"No."

"Too hot, eh?"

"I suppose so."

"What did you do, then?"

I try to smile, to look untroubled.

"What do you mean?" I ask.

"What did you do while I was sleeping?"

"I really don't remember," I tell her. "It was a while ago now, Prue. It was, what, a couple of decades ago."

"I remember it as if it was yesterday," she says keenly. "Every moment. Every second. I even remember the sensation of being asleep. Come on, Judith, you must remember. What did you do while I slept next to you?"

"I don't remember."

"It's important."

"Why?"

She opens her mouth to reply, but then something holds her back.

"I don't know," she says finally, sounding a little plaintive. "Honestly, I don't. It just feels as if it's very important indeed. The question is buzzing around in my head and I can't ignore it. Are you sure you don't remember, Judith? It was when the heat was really at its worst."

"If I could remember," I reply, "I would tell you."

As I say those words, in my mind's eye I see myself holding the rock up and then bashing it down against Prue's face. I didn't strike her, of course, but I think I *did* briefly hold the rock. And I felt as if I was being watched, too. I remember looking over at the tree-line and searching for an observer. I cannot tell any of that to Prue, of course, but I think I remember every moment of that walk. Even if I have, ever since, been trying to put it out of my mind.

"You must think that I'm a fool," she says suddenly.

"Not at all."

"Of course you do. I show up here, after all these years, babbling away about some old day that means nothing."

She smiles, but she looks distinctly uncomfortable, and then she gets to her feet.

"I have disturbed you for long enough," she says, as if she suddenly has a great urge to leave. "It was nice to see you again, Judith. You seem to be doing well and your daughter is absolutely delightful."

"It was nice to see you to," I reply, and I follow as she heads to the door. "Please have a safe -"

"I'm around later," she says suddenly,

turning to me.

"I beg your pardon?"

"I'm staying at the Hog and Bucket," she says cautiously. "I shall be eating my supper there tonight. I don't suppose you happen to be going there later, do you?"

"I never set foot in that place," I reply.

"Too down-market for you, is it?"

"It's really not my sort of establishment. There are far too many drunkards."

"I suppose so," she replies. "There wasn't really anywhere else to stay in Briarwych, though." She pauses. "If you change your mind and would like to talk some more, you know where to find me. We can even meet somewhere else, if you like."

"It was nice to see you," I tell her, "but I'm afraid I really am far too busy. Have a safe journey."

"You don't still have that crucifix, do you? The one that I found that day."

"I don't know where it might be," I lie. "I'm sorry."

"It's fine." She mutters something else under her breath, then she turns and makes her way out of the door. "It doesn't matter."

Breathing a sigh of relief once she's gone, I step across the hallway and gently push the door shut. I should not have been so troubled by her visit, but something about Prue Williams just makes me feel uncomfortable. Perhaps she is a reminder of a darker time in my life, of a moment that I have put in my past. For a moment I worry that her arrival cannot be a coincidence, not coming so soon after that voice that I heard, but then I tell myself to put some concerns to bed. And then, slowly, I look up the stairs as I realize that there is one thing I must check.

***

"If you really *must* remember the afternoon in the forest," the voice told me yesterday," the answer can be found wrapped in linen in the bottom drawer of your chest. The one in your bedroom. You put this answer there yourself. But do not torment yourself, Judith. I think it would upset you to know the truth. Simply be glad that the girl has learned her lesson."

Crouching in front of my dresser, I realize that I have delayed this moment for long enough. I pull the bottom drawer open, and then I start gently moving the bed-sheets aside. And then, just as I am beginning to think that there is nothing untoward here, I see that a piece of linen has been placed carefully in one of the corners, and it is quite clear that something is wrapped inside.

My heart is racing, but I force myself to reach out toward the item.

Suddenly I feel a rush of panic. I try to brace myself, but the sensation builds and builds until I fall back and bump against the side of my bed. I hold my hands up, as if to protect myself, as wave after wave of sheer dread comes rushing through my soul. I turn away and cry out, but for a moment it is as if the panic has seized me and will never let go. Only after a few more seconds does the feeling finally begin to fade, and I am left panting in shock on the bedrooms floor.

I look back toward the drawer. For a moment I consider looking again, but then I reach out with my right foot and push the drawer shut. There's nothing in there, anyway. I'm just letting myself get spooked. I need to get on with things, rather than allow myself to fall victim to these base superstitions.

CHAPTER ELEVEN

"MUMMY, NO!" ELIZABETH SCREAMS, twisting to get away from me. "Mummy, please!"

Grabbing her by the arm, I pull her back and put a hand over her mouth to keep her from crying out. Then, as she struggles some more, I reach down and put my other hand on her waist. Tears are streaming down her face and running onto my fingers, but my usual compassion is being pushed aside by a cold, hard anger. Reaching out, I grab the -

"No!" I gasp, suddenly opening my eyes and sitting up in bed.

My heart is racing, but I feel a rush of relief as I realize that I was merely having a nightmare. I dreamed I was in the forest with Elizabeth; I had her pinned down and I was determined to punish her, and I was filled with an anger that I have never felt in real life. I could sense something awful approaching, something utterly dreadful, and I cannot help but feel relieved that I woke before I reached that part of the nightmare.

As I try to gather my thoughts, my gaze falls upon the bottom drawer of the dresser. For a moment I contemplate the piece of linen that rests in there, and I find myself wondering what is wrapped inside the linen. I tell myself that I should not be concerned by such things, but then I cautiously climb out of bed and make my way over. Last night I experienced some kind of panic when I was about to unwrap the piece of linen, but this time I am sure I shall be a little stronger.

Reaching down, I begin to slide the drawer open.

I freeze as I see that, while the linen remains where I left it, there is now a small, dark red patch on the fabric, as if something bloodied has begun to soak through.

I hesitate for a moment, before sliding the drawer shut again. There is no rush to unwrap that piece of linen. I can do it tonight.

***

"I'm late," I say as I hurry down the stairs a few minutes later, having dressed in haste. "Elizabeth, why didn't you wake me? It's quarter past nine!"

Heading through to the kitchen, I spot Elizabeth sitting at the table with a rather strange, rather blank expression on her face. I make my way to the sink and pour myself a glass of water, and then I turn to see that Elizabeth is simply staring into space, and that her eyes look reddish and sore, as if she has been sobbing.

"Elizabeth?" I continue. "Are you okay? Why aren't you at school?"

She turns to me, but it takes a few more seconds before she seems to realize that I am here.

"I didn't feel well," she whispers.

"And what exactly is wrong?"

She swallows.

"Elizabeth, do you need to see a doctor?" I ask.

She pauses, before slowly shaking her head.

"Well, what's wrong?" I continue. "Elizabeth, you're starting to worry me."

"I think I just need to rest," she replies. "It'll pass in a day or two, I'm sure. Is that alright, Mother? I'll just go to bed and sleep until I feel better."

"I'm really not sure that sleep is the best thing," I tell her, before realizing that perhaps getting a doctor involved would not be the best idea. After all, there is still a part of me that worries about whatever happened in the forest, and that would rather let things resolve themselves without outside intervention. "A few more days, then," I tell her. "Then we'll have to reconsider."

She nods.

"And I must get to the church," I continue, hurrying to the door. "There's no -"

Stopping suddenly, I realize that something isn't quite right, and then I slowly turn and look at the back of Elizabeth's head.

"It's Saturday," I tell her.

I wait, but she doesn't answer.

"It's Saturday, Elizabeth," I continue. "There's no school on Saturday anyway."

"Oh." She pauses. "Okay, then."

I want to ask her what's really wrong, but I suppose she's just being a melodramatic young lady. I'm sure I merely told her off in the forest, and she's feeling a little glum about the whole thing. Rather than risk disturbing her further, then, I turn and hurry through to the hallway, and then I make my way out of the cottage and along the lane.

Reaching the cemetery, I open the gate and start making my way toward the church. One of the local tradesmen is busy digging a grave for Violet's funeral, but then I stop in my tracks as I see that Father Perkins is standing outside the church's main door.

And he is talking to Prudence Williams.

I step back behind one of the trees and

watch. I cannot hear from this distance what they are saying, but they seem to be deep in conversation. Father Perkins came to the parish long after Prue and her family moved away, so this is unlikely to be a reunion of old acquaintances, but I can think of no other reason why Prue would be here. She has never been a churchgoer and, indeed, I am not sure I have ever before seen her anywhere near a place of worship. Perhaps she is merely touring the local area, but I must confess that this whole situation seems rather odd. Prue's return to Briarwych is starting to make me a little unsettled.

Suddenly she turns and starts coming this way. I pull back out of sight and take care to remain unseen as she goes out through the gate. She is walking very swiftly, with great intent, and soon she is out of view. I turn and look back toward the church, but Father Perkins is also gone and I cannot shake the feeling that the conversation I just witnessed was not entirely pleasant.

I pause to gather my thoughts, and then I make my way along the path and into the church.

"Judith?" Father Perkins calls out from his office. "Is that you?"

I make my way over to the door and see that he is making tea. He looks rather flustered.

"I'm sorry I'm late," I tell him. "I shall make up the time."

"No, it's okay," he replies. "In fact, why

don't you take the day off? I'm sure you could spend some enjoyable time with Elizabeth."

"I have far too much to do here," I say, as I step into the room. "I must -"

Before I can finish, Father Perkins steps back, almost as if he is scared of me.

"Is anything the matter?" I ask.

He stares at me for a moment, as if he is waiting for something to happen, and then he manages a smile that seems rather forced.

"No, Judith," he says with a sigh, "nothing is the matter."

"What was Prudence Williams doing here?"

"Who?"

"The woman who was here a moment ago."

"There was no woman here a moment ago," he says, although he sounds a little tense. "You must be mistaken."

"Oh, but I saw -"

"There was no woman here," he says again. "I'm sorry, Judith, but there was no-one here so let's just let that be the end of it, eh? If you insist on working today, that is fine, but I have a great deal to do before Violet Durridge's funeral on Monday so I'm going to have to work in here. Please shut the door as you leave the office, and do not disturb me for the rest of the day."

I pause for a moment, feeling as if something is wrong, but then I realize that no good will come of forcing the matter.

"Of course," I say, turning to go back out into the corridor. At the last second, however, I spot an envelope resting on the table, and I see that my name is scrawled on the front in a crude, sloppy hand.

Reaching out, I pick the envelope up and turn it around, and I see that there seems to be a piece of paper inside.

"Where did this come from?" I ask.

"I'm sorry? Oh, yes, that had been slipped under the door when I woke up yesterday. I was going to give it to you, but I forgot."

I step out of the room and pull the door shut, and then I make my way along the corridor before stopping and opening the envelope. My hands are shaking a little, and I cannot escape the feeling that this envelope must be connected to Prue's sudden return, and perhaps to Father Perkins' insistence that the woman was not here a few minutes ago. And then, as I remove the slip of paper and turn it around, I feel a sliver of fear in my chest as I read the five words that are written on the page:

I know what you did.

CHAPTER TWELVE

"DEAR LORD, GIVE ME guidance," I whisper as I kneel before the altar. "I feel as if the world is running out of control."

It is late in the afternoon and I have spent the day in a frenzy. I have tried to distract myself with work, but finally I have decided to pray for help. There is no doubt that Prue has come to Briarwych with some kind of mischief in mind, and I cannot help but worry that somehow she saw me holding the rock all those years ago, that she knows I experienced that strange moment of temptation. And if she means to cause trouble, my entire reputation here in Briarwych could be damaged.

"Help me," I continue, with my eyes squeezed tight shut. "Guide me, Lord. I do not know what to do."

I wait, and the church remains silent.

Father Perkins is in his office still, with the door shut.

Finally, slowly, I open my eyes.

"Are you there?" I whisper, feeling a flicker of fear in my chest as the words leave my lips. "Are *you* listening?"

I wait.

"Of course I am here," the voice says suddenly. "I have heard every word you have uttered, but I thought you no longer wanted to hear me."

I look around, but there is still no sign of anybody standing nearby. I hesitate, worried in case this is all a trick, and then I turn back to look at the altar. I know I should not be interrupting my prayer to speak to this other voice, but I need help from somewhere.

"What does she want with me?" I ask.

"Who?"

"Prudence."

"She was here earlier, talking to the priest."

"What did she say?"

"She was talking about you, Judith."

I swallow hard.

"She told him that you should not be allowed in the church," the voice continues, "and that something was very wrong with you. He defended you at first, but she was very persuasive.

She has a snake's tongue when she speaks, and gradually she made him fearful. By the time she left, she had filled his mind with doubts."

"Why?" I ask. "What exactly did she tell him?"

"There is only one way for you to learn that, Judith," the voice says. "You know what you have to do."

***

As soon as I step through the door of the Hog and Bucket public house, I am overcome by the stench of beer. Every fiber of my being is urging me to leave this filthy place, but I force myself to walk toward the bar. There are drunkards all around, in various stages of inebriation, and I am quite aware that I am being watched. I am sure the locals never thought the day would come when they would see me in here.

"Good evening, Ms. Prendergast," Thomas Neill says, clearly amused by my arrival. "Come for a swift libation, have you?"

"Most certainly not," I reply, as the barman comes over. "I believe you have a guest, a Ms. Williams. Is she still here?"

"She's up in her room, I think," the barman replies. "She's been up there most of the day."

"I should like to speak to her."

"Stairs are near the toilets," he continues. "You'll find your way easily enough. She's in the first room."

"Thank you." With that, I turn to walk away.

"Funny," he adds, "she said you might be popping by, but I never believed her. Old friends of yours, is she?"

I glance back at him, but there is no point explaining anything to the ruffians in this place. Instead, I simply make my way toward a door at the far end of the room, and then I step through and see a set of narrow, twisting stairs. I start walking up, while still fighting against the desire to turn around and run. By the time I get to the top of the stairs, I feel as if my gut has been tied into knots, but I know that I must do this. Rather than give myself any more time to deliberate, I walk to the first door and knock.

"Come in," Prue calls out.

I take a deep breath, and then I push the door open and see that she is sitting at a desk by the window, writing in what looks like some kind of journal.

"Judith," she says after a moment, without looking at me, "what a pleasant surprise. I wasn't sure that you'd come."

I pause, before stepping into the room and shutting the door.

"I called round to the church this morning," she continues. "I hoped you might be there, but apparently you were late. What's wrong? Did you oversleep?" Finally she looks at me. "Bad dreams?"

"What do you want?" I ask.

"That's a rather broad question, Judith."

"Why are you here?" I ask. "What do you want with me?"

She stares at me for a moment, before setting her pen down. I wait, but now she's simply watching me, and I am starting to feel a little uncomfortable.

"You hear her, don't you?" she says finally. "I know you do. You hear her too."

"What do you -"

"Shaltak."

I flinch at the sound of that name.

"Something changed on that hot day," she continues. "I don't know what happened, not exactly, but I haven't been the same since and I think you haven't either. And then, recently, I began to hear this voice. I thought I was going mad at first, but the voice kept speaking and over time it proved itself to me. I asked it what it wanted, and it was a little cryptic for a while. Eventually, however, it started asking me if I remembered *you*."

"I don't know what you're talking about," I tell her.

"I think you do."

I shake my head.

"She didn't *tell* me to come back to Briarwych," she explains, "not in so many words, but the implication was there. I didn't understand at first, but when I saw you in your kitchen, I spotted something familiar in your eyes. I spotted the same fear I've seen in my own features, and in that instant I knew – I absolutely knew for certain – that you too have been hearing Shaltak's voice."

"I don't know what you're talking about," I say, turning and reaching out to open the door again. "Whatever you think is happening here, you're quite mistaken."

"You have such a lovely daughter."

I hesitate, with my hand on the doorknob.

"Lovely, but troubled," Prue continues. "It's the eyes, again. I know this is a cliche, but the eyes really *are* a way to see into the soul. Your daughter looks troubled by something and I think this something is fairly new. What happened to her?"

"Nothing," I reply. "She's -"

"What's in the bottom drawer of your dresser, Judith?"

I turn to her.

"Don't ask how I know that there's something there," she says. "You know how. Shaltak told me. She also told me that you're too scared to look."

"This is none of your business," I reply.

"We're two peas in the same pod right now, Judith," she continues, keeping her gaze fixed on me with uncommon intensity. "We have to work together to figure this out, or I'm scared we'll end up losing our minds. I'm so glad that you hear the voice too, because it means I'm not crazy, but we have to work out what it wants."

She gets to her feet and starts coming toward me.

"What did we do on that day, to attract its attention?" she asks. "What does it want from us?"

"I don't know what you mean," I say firmly.

"The voice is -"

"I have heard no voice," I tell her. "None of what you're saying makes sense."

"Deny it all you want," she replies, "but I know the truth. The voice is talking to both of us, I think it wants us to work together. I think we have to talk to it as one."

I shake my head.

"I can't do this alone," she continues, with a hint of desperation in her voice now. "I'm not asking you, Judith. I'm *begging* you. I think this voice is going to destroy us both unless we find a way to stand up to it. It's been watching us, Judith, and studying us ever since that baking hot day. Bad things have happened in my life, and I'm starting to wonder whether those bad things were caused by this voice, whether it somehow -"

"That's impossible," I reply, interrupting her.

"Is it? What if this thing has been manipulating us all along? What if it has been guiding us to this moment? We can't let it divide us, Judith. We have to take a stand. We're not strong enough unless we do this together."

Staring at her, I realize I can see true madness in her eyes. She's on the verge of breaking down, and I am shocked by the realization that she has allowed to get herself to such a state. At the same time, this realization serves to make *me* feel stronger, for I know that I cannot allow myself to do the same thing.

"I should not have come here tonight," I tell her finally. "I'm sorry, Prue, but I can't help you. I hear no voice. And now, I would be grateful if you would leave me alone. Do not come to my home again, do not come to the church, do not spread rumors about me. You are wrong and -"

"Judith, please..."

"You are wrong!" I snap. "Can you get that through your thick head? Whatever is happening to you, it is most certainly not happening to me! I wish I could help you, but I can't."

I open the door and step out onto the landing, and now I can see sheer desperation in her eyes.

"I think you should leave Briarwych," I tell

her. “There's nothing for you here. If you try to contact me again, I shall have to consider going to the police. Whatever you want, you will not get it by harassing me. I bid you goodbye, Prue, and it pains me to say that I hope very much that I shall never see your face again.”

Turning, I head to the stairs. I half-expect her to come rushing after me, but thankfully she leaves me alone as I start making my way down to the ground floor. I think I hear her starting to sob in her room, but I force myself to keep going and I am actually rather relieved as I find myself back in the main room of the public house, where everybody seems rather merry and carefree.

For a moment, I stand and watch the drunkards, and I actually find myself admiring their ability to lose themselves so easily. Then, realizing that this is no time for such foolish thoughts, I make my way to the door. I ignore the few people who attempt to lure me into conversation, and I go outside into the dark street. Stopping, I look up at the windows and I see the there is still a light in Prue's room. Perhaps she is still sobbing up there, or perhaps she has pulled herself together. One thing is certain, however; I refuse to admit to her that I heard the voice.

The sooner Prue leaves me alone, the sooner things can start getting back to normal.

CHAPTER THIRTEEN

STANDING ALONE IN THE kitchen once I am home, I tell myself that this madness is finally starting to make sense. On the way home, I began to think about everything that has happened, and it occurred to me that perhaps I have missed one obvious explanation.

Prudence Williams has been setting me up.

The voice in the church did not sound particularly like her, but then again I suppose she might be capable of distorting her voice in some manner. The things she told me were striking, but – again – it is not impossible that she could have learned of certain matters. If she had been watching me, she would have easily noticed that I found Violet Durridge irritating. I am not quite ready to believe that she could have *killed* Violet, but she might have made an ill-time comment that happened to coincide with the terrible fire. And perhaps she was watching Elizabeth for a while, which is how she learned of her extra-curricular activities. And the voice...

I pause as I try to work out how she could have achieved the voice. Finally I realize that she must just be very good at secreting herself out of sight. Certainly I look around to see if anybody was nearby at the time, but I did not conduct an exhaustive search of every nook and cranny. The more I think of it, the more I am sure that I have been the victim of a madwoman. I can only hope that tonight I made her understand why this must all end, and now she will leave me alone.

Otherwise, I suppose I shall have to involve the police.

Realizing that I am utterly exhausted, I turn and make my way through to the hallway. I need to sleep, but as I reach the bottom of the stairs I realize I can hear a faint sobbing sound coming from up in Elizabeth's room. My first thought is incredulity and sorrow, at the thought that my dear daughter is still in such a terrible state, but then I realize that there is another sound as well. While the sobs continue, I can hear a faint thudding sound as well, and I listen for a moment as I try to discern what could possibly be causing this sound.

Finally, slowly, I start making my way very

quietly up the stairs.

As I reach the top, I hear another thud, except this time it sounds quicker and sharper somehow. Elizabeth is still sobbing, and I have to force myself to refrain from rushing into her room to find out whatever is the matter. I tell myself that I need to be cautious here, that I have to get to the root of whatever's happening, so I creep to the door and then stop again to listen.

Between the sobs, Elizabeth is whispering.

I feel an immediate rush of fear, at the thought that perhaps she too is hearing some kind of voice. After a few seconds, however, I realize that she seems to be apologizing for something, whimpering the word 'Sorry' over and over again. Then I hear her mention me, as if she's apologizing for something that has made me angry. And then, suddenly, I flinch as I hear a particularly loud thud and Elizabeth lets out a pained cry.

I can hold back no longer.

Opening the door, I hurry into her room, and then I scream as I see that she is kneeling on the floor with cuts and splits running all across her bloodied back.

"Elizabeth!" I gasp. "What -"

Before I can finish, she strikes herself again, flaying her own skin with strings of knotted cord tied to some kind of handle.

"No!" I shout, hurrying over and pulling the

cat o' nine tails from her hand.

She screams and lunges at me, desperately trying to grab the weapon back, but then she looks into my eyes and I see a moment of recognition. She hesitates, and then she pulls back and grabs her bed-sheets, pulling them down to cover her wounds as she retreats into the far corner of the room.

"What are you doing?" I ask, holding the cat o' nine tails in my trembling hand. Looking down at the knotted cords, I see that they are dripping blood.

"I'm bad!" she sobs. "What I did was bad!"

"No!" I stammer, before throwing the whip out of the room and then hurrying over to kneel next to Elizabeth. "My darling, I -"

"Don't touch me!" she screams, turning away. Blood is already soaking through the bed-sheets. "Don't look at me!"

"Why are you doing this to yourself?" I ask, with tears in my eyes. "Elizabeth, whatever has possessed you?"

I pause for a moment, staring at her horrified face. At first I tell myself that I have never seen her look quite *this* upset before, but then I realize that I have seen her sobbing and wailing in my nightmares. She is my darling girl, and at this moment she looks like a terrified animal.

"You told me," she whimpers. "I did a bad thing and I have to pay. You punished me in the forest, but then I kept catching myself having bad thoughts so I decide to punish myself some more."

"I didn't do this to you," I tell her, and now the tears are running down my face. "I would never do this to you, Elizabeth."

"I'm a coward," she sobs. "I made the whip myself. I should have done what you did to me, but I didn't dare. I tried and tried, but I just..."

She breaks into a series of wailing cries. I instinctively rush forward to console her, but she screams and rushes away, scrambling across the room and then clambering onto the bed. She leaves smeared blood in her wake, and I'm horrified to see that there's more blood all over her pajama bottoms. As she cowers next to the pillows and stares at me with terrified eyes, I feel my heart shatter into a thousand pieces.

"It's going to be alright," I tell her, my voice trembling with shock. "I will fix this. I don't know how, not yet, but I will fix everything."

Slowly, I reach a hand toward her.

She immediately flinches and pulls back.

I hesitate, before lowering my hand and then getting to my feet. I feel utterly horrified, and my mind is racing as I try to work out how I'm going to make everything okay again. My knees are trembling and I have to stop for a moment in the doorway to steady myself, and I stand for a moment listening to the sound of Elizabeth still sobbing on the bed.

I don't know how I'm going to fix this.

No.

Wait.

I do.

I take a deep breath as my chest tightens with fear. I want there to be another way, *any* other way, but time is running out and I'll do anything to calm my dear daughter down.

"Wait here," I say calmly, as Elizabeth continues to sob. "I have to go out for a few minutes. When I get back, everything will be alright again. I promise."

I start turning to look at her, but at the last moment I stop myself. I know what I'll see; I'll see my terrified, weeping, bleeding daughter again. The next time I see her, I want her to look happy and carefree, and she *will* be that way, I'm certain. First, though, I must strike a deal.

"You're real, aren't you?" I whisper.

I wait.

"Come to the church," the voice replies.

A shudder runs through my body. I had managed to convince myself that the voice was all Prue's doing, but now I know that I was wrong. The voice is real, and it is waiting for me. The voice will help Elizabeth, and in return I shall give it anything it wants. Even my life.

"I'll be back soon," I tell Elizabeth, before making my way down the stairs and then out of the house.

Outside, a full moon casts eerie blue light across the village. I walk along the lane, heading up the gentle slope that leads higher and higher up into the night. Finally, ahead against the dark sky, I spot the silhouette of Briarwych Church.

CHAPTER FOURTEEN

THE GATE CREAKS SLIGHTLY as I swing it open. I can see my own breath in the cold night air as I hurry along the path that leads to the church. All the lights are off, and I know Father Perkins will be asleep by now. I don't know how I am going to speak to the voice without Father Perkins hearing, but I shall have to find a way. All that matters is reaching the altar and begging the voice for help.

"Hello, Judith," Prue says suddenly, stepping out from behind one of the trees and stopping in my path, "fancy seeing you here."

"I don't have time for -"

"I know, I know," she says, blocking me as I try to step past her, "you've come to ask the voice for help. It's about your daughter, isn't it?"

She grabs my right wrist, as if to hold me

here.

"Shaltak already told me everything. She told me you'd be here soon. She even told me about that afternoon in the forest with your daughter. Tell me, Judith, have you looked in your bottom dresser drawer yet?"

"I have no time for this," I tell her firmly, as I try to pull free of her grip. "Get out of my way or I'll -"

"Or you'll what?" she snaps. "Scream? Attract attention? Make people start gossiping about you again?"

"I'm going into that church," I reply, "and you can't stop me."

"Judith, you -"

"Get out of my way!" I hiss, pulling free and storming past her. "I'm not -"

Before I can finish, she clamps a hand over my mouth from behind and pulls me down onto my knees. I try to twist free, but suddenly I feel something sharp pressing against my throat and I realize that she's holding a knife.

"I tried to play nice with you tonight," she whispers, her hot breath rushing into my ear, "but you turned me down. And after that is when I realized the truth. Shaltak didn't pick both of us that day. She decided to play us off against one another, to see who's stronger." She presses the blade more firmly against my throat. "But here's the thing,

Judith. She always knew that I'd turn out to be the strongest. She gave you a chance, but it was always going to be me. It took a while, but I finally came for you, and now I'm going to finish this."

I try again to pull away, but she's holding me too tight. I try to scream, but her hand remains clamped firmly over my mouth.

"The best part," she continues, "is that there's already a grave dug here, so I can just toss you in and cover you with some dirt. Do you think anyone's going to miss you, Judith? I doubt they'll bother to search too long. Even your daughter will probably be glad to see the back of you."

She runs the blade against my throat, but I don't think she's cut me just yet. I don't feel any blood.

"Goodbye, Judith," she sneers. "Your death will prove to Shaltak that I'm her only true -"

Slamming my head back, I manage to hit her in the face. We both fall back and, somehow, the knife fails to cut my throat. I push her arm away and try to grab the knife, but she's holding it too tight and after a moment she lunges at me and bites hard on the side of my neck. I let out a pained cry as I continue to try wrestling the knife from her grip, but I can already feel blood running down to my collarbone. I start scratching her wrist, hoping that the pain will make her let go of the knife's handle, but suddenly she pushes me aside and rolls onto me, while freeing her hand and raising the knife high against the night sky.

Without saying another word, she slams the knife down toward my face. I manage to slip a hand free and grab her wrist, stopping her just as the blade is about to reach my left eye. I struggle for a moment to keep the knife away, and then I start slowing twisting the blade around so that it's no longer aimed at my face.

“When are you going to realize that it's over?” she snarls. “Shaltak wants me, not you! You're pathetic, Judith! People won't even remember you round here! They sense the evil in your soul and they're starting to hate you more than ever!”

I try to push her away, but I can't. Instead, she starts pressing the knife down toward my chest. My left hand is still trying to turn the blade to the side, while my right hand is pushing as hard as I can against Prue's shoulder. I can already feel myself getting weaker, and I know Prue will soon manage to drive the blade into my body. I look around, desperately hoping that I might be able to get away, and then at the last moment I spot a rock on the ground next to one of the graves.

Letting go of Prue's hand, I grab the rock and then swing it straight at her head, smashing her on the temple and sending her crumpling to the ground.

I spot the blade flashing in the moonlight, but I don't give her time to attack me again. Instead, I bring the rock crashing down against her head for a second time. I see and hear and feel her skull cracking with a dull thud. She lets out a pained groan and her body jerks slightly, but I'm already raising the rock again. This time, I bring it down against her eye, obliterating the socket and sending blood splattering out across the moonlit grass. I raise the rock yet again and watch for a moment as more blood bursts out from between broken sheets of bone, and then I smash the rock over and over against Prue's face until all that is left is a bloodied mess. Then I keep going, aiming at the top of her neck, hitting her and not even caring when blood sprays against my face. I work myself into a frenzy, bashing her head until finally my hands seize up and I drop the rock, and I see that I have bashed Prue's head clear away from her shoulders.

Just like...

I pause for a moment, before dropping the rock and pulling back.

I wait, in case this all turns out to be a nightmare, but this time Prue seems to be really dead. It all happened exactly as I hallucinated it before, except that this time it seems there shall be no miraculous reversal.

"You surprise me," Shaltak's voice says after a moment, whispering in my mind. "I felt sure that she would be the victor."

"I didn't do this," I stammer, as I feel panic welling in my body. "I didn't, I mean, I couldn't have, I..."

My voice trails off as I realize that, all these years later, I have finally made good on the dark promise of that summer's day.

"Come to me," Shaltak continues. "The priest is sleeping, and I shall ensure that he does not wake until we are done. We need to discuss your future, Judith. We need to have the conversation that I had expected to have with Prudence."

"I don't want to be..."

I pause for a moment, and then I stumble to my feet.

"Elizabeth," I whisper.

"Come into the church," Shaltak says, "and everything will become clear."

***

Father Perkins sniffs and snorts as he rolls over in bed, and then he starts snoring again. I watch for a moment, before gently bumping the door shut.

"I told you," Shaltak says, "I'll make sure that he sleeps through the night."

Turning, I head across the corridor and then alone the aisle, making my way toward the altar. Although I cannot help but relive the moment of

Prue's death over and over, I feel strangely calm; I am not trembling or shaking, or weeping, and I feel no fear as I reach the far end of the aisle and look up at the high, beautiful stained-glass window that rises high above. For a few precious seconds, the sheer beauty of Briarwych Church is enough to fill my soul with wonder, until I remember why I came here tonight.

"You have hidden depths," Shaltak says. "You might not look strong, Judith, but you possess something extraordinary. You have an ability to exceed your capabilities. You continue to grow, to develop. Your potential has not yet been reached, which excites me. Together, Judith, you and I can go far."

"I want my daughter to be safe," I reply.

"Is she not safe now?"

"Something's wrong with her. I don't know what, not exactly, but she's suffering and I want that to end." I wait, but Shaltak says nothing. "I'll give you anything," I continue, "but only on the condition that Elizabeth is safe. And that she's with me."

"What do you offer in return?"

I take a deep breath.

"What do you want?" I ask.

"I want the one thing that you possess, that I do not."

"I don't know what that is." Again, I wait for

an answer. "My soul?" I ask finally. "Is it my soul that you want?"

"You think I don't have a soul?" She laughs. "I have more than enough of a soul, Judith. What I lack, in your mortal world, is a body."

"You want a body?" I ask, before realizing what she meant. "You want *my* body?"

"We can share. I have been in your body a few times already, mostly staying quiet and journeying with you. I want to become more a part of you, so that I can feel what it is like to be human. Once I have done that, I shall be able to manifest my own body. That manifestation is the easy part. I just need some experience first, so that I know what I must create."

"And then what will you do?"

"I honestly haven't decided."

"But you're not..."

I hesitate to say the word.

"You're not a demon, are you?" I say cautiously. "I know I've asked you that before, but I'm still not sure what your answer meant. I can't make a pact with a demon, I just... I can't!"

"I am whatever you want me to be, Judith," she replies. "Your words mean nothing to me. But I will help you, and I will do what I can to save your daughter, and on that you have my promise. I hope that will be enough for you, and that over time we shall be able to cooperate a little more fully. I need to learn from you. I need to know what it feels like to have a body again, to be alive. Will you help me with that?"

I pause for a moment, before nodding.

"I will," I tell her. "For Elizabeth."

"Then you shall find her mind calmed upon your return," Shaltak explains. "It will take time for her to recover entirely, but she is already strong. In some ways, she is like you. She is defiant."

"I should go to her," I reply, taking a step back. "I want to be with her."

"Of course," Shaltak says, "although there is one other matter to which you should attend first."

"What's that?" I ask. "Please, I want to get home to my daughter. Can't this other matter wait until tomorrow?"

***

A few minutes later, I finally manage to roll Prue's body into the grave that has been dug for Violet Durridge. Hurrying back across the moonlit cemetery, I grab the other body parts and then I throw those into the grave as well, and then I grab a shovel and start covering the corpse with soil. It takes a while, but finally Prue's body has been completely covered and I step back in an attempt to catch my breath.

Now I can go home to Elizabeth.

CHAPTER FIFTEEN

"AND WE ASK THAT you take Violet into your kingdom, Lord," Father Perkins says, as a light rain continues to fall, "and that she is granted the rewards of her life here in our community. Amen."

"Amen," I whisper, but I am the only one.

It is shocking indeed that nobody else has come to pay their respects to Violet, but I suppose I should not really be quite so surprised. Briarwych is a quiet place at the best of times, and I have often noticed a certain coldness in the people here. Besides, those who wish to mark Violet's passing will probably prefer to do so at the Hog and Bucket, where they can drink beer after beer and remember her in their own manner. I had thought that one or two of them might come to the funeral, but evidently this is not to be.

Looking down into the grave, at the coffin which has already been lowered into place, I briefly think back to the other night, when I buried Prue in that same space. Now, with the groundsman about to start filling the grave in, the secret of Prue's death looks set to be hidden forever.

"I must confess," Father Perkins says as he comes over to join me, "to a certain sense of melancholy on this sad occasion. Nobody's funeral should be so sparsely attended."

"We make our own lives," I remind him. "Perhaps this day should be a warning to all of us." I turn to him. "I know this might be rather forward of me, Father," I continue, "but would you like to come to have tea with Elizabeth and me one evening? We would be more than happy to set an extra space for you at the table."

He opens his mouth to reply, but he seems a little hesitant. Indeed, he has seemed rather reluctant ever since I spotted him speaking to Prue the other day. I can only imagine the lies and half-truths she must have told him, but I am confident that I can win him over again. With a little patience, I believe I shall be the wife of a priest yet.

"One evening, maybe," he says cautiously. "Thank you for your kind offer, Ms. Prendergast."

"Call me Judith," I remind him. "You have done in the past."

"I should go inside and get back to work,"

he says with a sigh, as the rain seems to intensify a little. "This is not the day for being outdoors, is it? I don't know about you, but I intend to go inside, make a nice cup of tea, and perhaps read for a while before I start writing a few letters."

With that, he heads into the church. I stand at the grave for a moment longer, watching as the groundsman dumps another shovelful of soil onto the coffin. He's employing the same shovel that I used a couple of nights ago, and after a moment I look down and see that already the coffin is starting to get covered. As the groundsman works, he has no idea that he is filling not one grave, but two.

***

"I'm afraid that it was a very sad affair," I tell Elizabeth as I head over to the kitchen table. "One must be mindful of these things. Some lives might seem enjoyable, but they are frivolous and they do not, in the end, contribute anything of worth to society. Why, I imagine that within a few years the name Violet Durridge will have been completely forgotten."

I take an apple from the bowl, and then I glance at Elizabeth as she watches me from the doorway. I allow myself a faint smile as I see that, just as Shaltak promised, she has rather straightened herself up and recovered from her woes of last week. Soon she'll be back to normal and ready to go to school again.

"What is it?" I ask, aware that there's a slightly odd look on her face. "Elizabeth, what's wrong?"

"You're different," she replies.

"I am?"

"You're very different," she continues, as I take a bite from the apple. "I don't know what it is, Mother, but you seem so much more at ease with yourself. Did something happen?"

"Not that I can think of," I tell her. "Perhaps there has been a change in the air, that's all. One never knows, does one?"

Smiling, I head over to the sink, but then I glance at Elizabeth as I realize that she is still watching me.

"Whatever is the matter, darling?" I ask, worrying slightly that she might be suffering a relapse. "You know you can tell me, don't you?"

"I just..."

She pauses, and then she smiles and that strange look is gone.

"It's nothing," she says, "I'm sure I was just reading too much into it. I think I might go to my room now and read, ready for school later in the week. That's okay, isn't it?"

"Of course," I tell her. "You're very studious."

She turns and walks away, and I can't help but notice that she still has that very faint limp that I first noticed last week. I haven't wanted to pry too much, but at the same time I cannot help but wonder how and when she picked up some extra little injury. Deep down, I am worried that this injury might be related to that afternoon in the forest when I caught up to her, although I know I would never have actually hurt her. I scolded her, perhaps, but I would never have actually caused her any physical harm.

And then I remember the linen in the dresser, and I realize that I have delayed looking for so very long. If I am ever to look at all, this should be the moment.

I still hesitate, as if something is holding me back, but then I turn and head through to the hallway. Once I'm at the top of the stairs, I stop for a moment and listen, and sure enough I hear Elizabeth saying her times tables out loud. Satisfied that she's busy, I go through to my room and gently shut the door, and then I kneel before the dresser. Opening the bottom drawer, I immediately see the piece of linen, and I can't help but notice that the bloodstain seems to be very slightly larger.

I glance once more toward the landing.

"Six times seven is forty-two," I hear Elizabeth saying. "Seven times seven is forty-nine."

Good. She is still doing her homework, like

a good girl.

Slowly, I reach into the drawer and lift out the piece of linen. Whatever's wrapped inside is not heavy at all. I place the linen on the floor and then – despite the growing sense of fear in my heart – I begin to pull the layers aside, until finally I see a single red rose resting on the bloodied white fabric.

For a moment, this sight is something of a relief.

Then I notice the blood that is smeared all over the stem.

Peering closer, I see that there are small, dark strands stuck to many of the thorns. I touch one of the strands with a fingertip and find that it is slightly soft, like...

In that instant, I remember everything.

"Mummy, no!" Elizabeth screamed in the forest that day, as I held her down.

"Is this what was so important?" I shouted at her, as I held up the very same rose, which she had been carrying away from her meeting with the strange man. "Is this the only thing that matters to you?"

She continued to scream, but somehow I was too strong for her. I remember being filled with rage, with a kind of unholy anger that felt as if it was being channeled into my body. I remember reaching down and pulling Elizabeth's dress up, then pulling her underwear down, then turning the rose stem around so that the cut end was pointing at her body.

And then...

Unable to comprehend the true horror of what I did that day, I stare down at the rose as I sit in my bedroom. I stare in particular at the small strands of torn, bloodied flesh that still cling to the thorns. For a few seconds my entire body is still, but then the horror bursts through my soul and I let out an anguished gasp as I fall back and bump against the side of my bed, with the rose still in my hands.

My darling girl.

How could I have done something like that to her?

Her agonized, juddering screams ring out in my memory, just as they rang out in the forest. At the same time, I remember how she staggered home. I made her go before me, and I felt no compassion as she stumbled several times and almost fell. I hear my voice, commanding her to always remember her sins, to remember that sins can never be washed away, that they build up and build up in one's soul over a lifetime. She was sobbing, whimpering so loudly, but I would not let her stop. I made her walk all the way home.

Getting to my feet, I stare down at the rose for a moment before suddenly letting it fall from my hands. I step back, horrified by the sight of the perverted thing as it drops onto the carpet, and then

I back out onto the landing. I feel as if an immense surge of horror and pain is going to burst through my body at any moment. I have to stop that surge, and so I hurry over to Elizabeth's door and – without knocking – I push it open.

"Three times eight is twenty-four," she says as she sits at her desk. "Four times eight is -"

"Oh my darling!" I shout, rushing forward and dropping to my knees, then putting my arms around her and hugging her as tight as I can manage. "I don't know what came over me! I am so sorry!"

Sobbing, I rest my head on her shoulder.

"Four times eight is thirty-two," she continues after a moment. "Five times eight is forty."

Pulling back, I see that she is still looking at her schoolbooks. Her eyes are tear-free, and a few seconds later she turns to me and smiles.

"It's alright, Mother," she says calmly. "You were right. I deserved it."

"No," I reply, shaking my head. "No, my darling, what I did was abominable! What I did was unforgivable!"

"I deserved worse," she continues. "You helped put me back onto the right path, but it is my task to *walk* that path. I am going to keep myself honest from now on. You do not need to worry."

"Your injuries," I stammer, "they..."

I cannot even say the words.

"They'll heal," she says, as if this is a matter of no great importance. "There'll be scars, I hope. I want to always be reminded of the lesson you taught me."

"I am a monster," I tell her. "I have done such wicked things to you."

"You're my mother and I love you," she says, as her smile remains. Then, suddenly, she leans forward and kisses me briefly on the cheek, before pulling back again. "There," she adds. "Do you feel better now? You should be glad that your chastisement worked. I have put away my foolishness. Everything is going to be okay again."

I wait for her to say that she understands, or that she hates me, for her to say anything at all. Instead, she stares at me as if I'm making a fuss over nothing, and after a moment her smile grows.

"You're a silly goose, Mummy," she says finally. "Stop worrying so much."

"But I..."

For a moment, I cannot believe that she is so calm. What I did to her was inexcusable, yet she is acting as if I merely gave her an admonishing glance. I want to beg her to forgive me, but she already *has* forgiven me, and far too easily.

"Might I continue with my work?" she asks. "I'm sorry, but I've already missed rather a lot of school over the past week and I'm keen to catch up.

I'd hate to fall too far behind."

I open my mouth to tell her that this reaction is wrong, but then I realize that there is no point. She seems utterly lost in her own thoughts, and I think I know why this is the case.

"I must go out for a while," I tell her, stepping back to the doorway. "You will be fine here, I trust?"

"Of course, Mummy," she replies breezily, as if she has not a care in the world. "Why wouldn't I be?"

CHAPTER SIXTEEN

RUSHING INTO THE CEMETERY, I begin to make my way along the path that leads to the church's main door. Evening light is fading now, and the cemetery is bathed in the dull blue-tinted glow of approaching evening. My heart is racing, but I know that I must go to Shaltak and beg for her help. Something is desperately wrong with Elizabeth.

Suddenly I trip and stumble, before falling hard onto my knees. I let out a pained wince before starting to get up, but then I find that a figure is towering over me.

I scream as I see a headless woman wearing Prue's dress.

"No!" I shout, turning away and cowering for a moment. "Leave me alone!"

I wait, and then I turn to see that the figure is gone. I look around, but I am all alone in the cemetery, and I hurry to my feet and race to the church before the figure can appear again.

***

"Father Perkins?" I call out as soon as I am in the church. "Father Perkins, are you here?"

I make my way to his office and look inside, but there is no sign of him, and after a moment I notice that his shoes and his bicycle are missing. Evidently he is out somewhere in the village, or perhaps at the airbase, so I make my way along the aisle until I reach the altar and then I hurriedly get down onto my knees.

"I need Elizabeth to be alright," I stammer desperately. "Something's wrong. Something's so very wrong."

"I thought you wanted her suffering to end," Shaltak replies. "Does she seems now as if she is suffering?"

"I want her to be alright again," I explain, "but not like this. What I did was terrible. She can't just accept it."

"Why not?"

"Because it's not right!" I shout. "It's not natural!"

"Let me get this straight, Judith," Shaltak

replies. "You now *want* Elizabeth to be shouting and crying?"

"I want her to react to this normally," I continue, "so that eventually she'll get over it. Pushing it down like this, rationalizing it... She can't live like this forever."

"You confuse me, Judith. First you ask for one thing, and then the other."

"I want to have never done this at all," I reply. "To have never done what I did to her in the forest."

"I cannot undo actions."

"I know," I say, "but..."

I try to work out how this can all be made better, but for a moment I can think of no solution.

"I am enjoying experiencing these emotions with you," Shaltak says. "Guilt. Shame. Shock. I am learning so much about how it feels to inhabit a human body. I can already tell that my time with you, Judith, is going to be very productive."

"Why did I do that to her?" I sob. "Even in my greatest fit of anger, I would never dream of hurting my girl, it's almost as if..."

Pausing, I feel a rippling sense of dread rising through my chest.

"It's almost as if I had been possessed," I say finally, as the truth becomes clear. "Was that really me in the forest, or were you controlling me? I barely remember anything that happened, it's as if

I experienced some form of mania. Nothing like that has ever happened to me before, so I am left to wonder..." I look up toward the altar. "Did you attack Elizabeth *through* me?"

"I might have helped unleash your true anger," she replies, "and I might have helped a little. It was a fun thing to experience, Judith. The rhythmic ripping sound of thorns against tender flesh, of -"

"No!" I shout, getting to my feet as I start shaking with rage. "How dare you? I hadn't even accepted your offer at that point! How dare you take control of my body and make me do such an awful things?" There are tears in my eyes now, and I am starting to clench my fists. "Get out," I add finally. "Get out of my body and get out of my head!"

"We have a deal, Judith."

"That was before I knew what you'd made me do!" I shout. "Get out of my life!"

She stares laughing.

Stepping back, I feel a rising sense of panic as I realize that I have made a terrible mistake. I have allowed a creature – a demon, no less – to influence the course of my life's events, and I do not know how to extricate myself from this horror. As Shaltak's laughter continues to ring out in my mind, I finally turn and start hurrying back along the aisle, only to stop again as I see a figure standing in the archway. For a moment it is too dark for me to make the figure out, but then I take another faltering step forward and see that Father Perkins is staring at me.

"I was just..."

My voice trails off as I realize that I have no idea how long he has spent watching. And listening.

"I'm sorry to have disturbed you, Father," I continue, desperately hoping that I can keep the truth from him while I try to work out what to do. "It's late, I know that," I stammer, stepping forward and trying to smile in an attempt to appear untroubled. "I just wanted to pray a little more than normal, that's all. I don't know about you, but sometimes the urge to pray comes into me at the most inopportune moments and..."

Again, my voice trails off.

Father Perkins is staring at me with an expression of shock.

"How... How long have you been standing here?" I ask finally.

"Who were you talking to just now?" he asks.

I swallow hard.

"Judith," he continues, "that did not sound like any prayer that I have ever heard before."

"Father, I was merely..."

I take a deep breath as I realize that perhaps Father Perkins can help me. I must prostrate myself before him and hope that he takes pity upon my wretched soul.

"I have made a terrible mistake," I continue, as tears start to fill my eyes. "I have convened with -"

Suddenly a great pain breaks in my chest. I stumble forward and let out a loud, ringing burp, and then I drop to my knees and have to steady myself against the side of a pew. I wait as the echo of the pain recedes, but I can already feel something truly unnatural stirring in my gut.

"I have made a mistake," I say, my voice tight now with the anticipation of fresh pain. "Father, I need to know what can be done. I have strayed from the Lord and wandered onto the path of -"

Again the pain rips through my body. This time I retch loudly and fall forward, and bile rushes into the back of my throat and then dribbles from my lips. I retch again, but fortunately nothing comes up, and after a moment I look up at Father Perkins as a terrible cramp starts to grow in my stomach.

"Help me!" I gasp.

"What have you done?" he asks.

I reach a hand toward him.

"Help me," I sob. "Please..."

"What have you done, Judith?" he says, taking a step back.

"It's inside me," I whimper, as the pain grows and grows. "It's my fault, I invited it in, and now it won't leave."

"She was right," he says, his eyes filled with fear. "That woman who came to the church the other day told me that you were in league with a demon. I defended you, I refused to believe it could be true even though she seemed most certain."

"She was in league too," I tell him. "I was stronger. It chose me. And now it wants to -"

Suddenly the pain explodes, but this time it pushes up through my body with such force that I inadvertently stumble to my feet and take a few steps forward. I rest again against another pew, but I already know that the pain is twisting and roiling in anticipation of another surge.

"I beg you to help me," I gasp, "and -"

Before I can finish, I start laughing. I do not know where the laughter comes from, but it fills my body with wave after wave. I try to cry out as the sensation burns through my agonized belly, but the laughter is too strong and finally I stumble toward Father Perkins while reaching out to him for help. He backs away, as if he is terrified of my touch, and finally he reaches the corridor and I stop to steady myself in the archway.

"Judith," he says cautiously, "I need to know exactly what you have done."

"I have sinned!" I scream, shocking myself. That was my voice, but there was something else in there, something much stronger and darker, as if my voice and Shaltak's spoke as one.

Father Perkins takes another step back, and it's clear that he noticed the change.

"Is that what you want to hear?" I snarl, as I feel my lips curling to form a smile despite the pain in my gut. "The Lord didn't answer me, so I found someone who would. At least Shaltak's not a fucking disgrace. At least Shaltak cares enough to do something!"

"Judith..."

"That wasn't me!" I blurt out, and now my voice is back to normal, albeit wracked with fear. "I swear, Father, that was the demon speaking through me."

"This isn't possible," he replies. "Judith Prendergast is a good woman and -"

"I *am* a good woman!" I splutter, before feeling my face twist into a fresh smile. "Do you want to go through to your bedroom," Shaltak asks through me, "and I'll show you just how good I can be?"

"In the name of the Lord -"

Suddenly the laughter explodes once again from my body, shaking me so hard that I almost fall to the floor. I manage to steady myself, but now the laughter is getting stronger and stronger and I fear that I shall be shaken apart. I am laughing so much, my stomach feels as if it might soon be ripped apart, and finally I turn and start stumbling toward the main door. Somehow I feel as if the laughter is directed specifically at Father Perkins, and that the pain might be eased a little if I can just get out of the church.

“Judith,” he says behind me, “you must pray to the Lord for salvation.”

“Leave me alone,” I whisper, struggling to get the door open.

“It is your only hope,” he continues. “You must beg the Lord -”

“Go to Hell!” I scream, turning to him. “Go wash your filthy hands in a muddy river, Father,” I continue, and now I can tell that Shaltak is once again speaking through me. “What twists of logic keep a holy man in a place like this, while a war rages? Are you a coward, Father? Are you content for the young and the strong and the poor to go and fight for what you believe in, while you yourself hide here in comfort?”

“I do more good here,” he stammers, clearly shocked. “I look after the people of -”

“These people don't need you!” I snarl. “They don't need anything! They're pathetic imbeciles and their lives will rumble along with or without a priest! Don't you think you'd be of more use out there, helping the soldiers? Deep down you know that I'm right. Fancy that, Father. A demon tells you a greater truth than your Lord will ever reveal to you. You prefer his soothing lies to the cold, hard reality."

He stares at me, and I can see that these words have shocked him to his core.

"Get back to your groveling, spineless prayers," my voice continues. "It's fine. I'm sure you'll still be able to convince yourself that you're doing the right thing. After all, I'm just a demon, aren't I? I couldn't possible be right about anything."

With that, I turn and stumble out into the cold night air. I can feel Shaltak in my thoughts, but at least I'm back in control of my own body. And as I run across the cemetery, I know that only one thing matters now. I have to find my darling Elizabeth.

***

"Elizabeth!" I shout as soon as I'm back in the house. "Elizabeth, I have to talk to you!"

I hurry through to the living room, then to the kitchen, and then I go over and stop at the foot of the stairs.

"Elizabeth, come down here!" I cry. "Hurry!"

I wait, but I don't hear her, so I make my way up the stairs and then I barge into her room, only to find that she's not here either. I turn to hurry back out, but at the last moment I spot what looks like a note on her desk, so I walk over and pick the piece of paper up, only to find that it contains a brief message:

I know what you did,
but I also know why you did it.
I'm wicked.
I'm going to go and become a better person.
I'll come back when I'm good.
I love you, Mummy.

The handwriting is messy and barely legible, as if it was written by someone in pain. I barely even recognize it as Elizabeth's writing at all, but slowly I begin to realize that perhaps she was struggling when she wrote this message. It's the same writing, more or less, as the note that was delivered to the church. I had assumed that was written by Prue, but evidently Elizabeth was already trying hard to deal with what happened in the forest.

"Where are you?" I whisper, suddenly panicking at the thought of my girl having run away from home.

Dropping the note, I start checking Elizabeth's cupboards and drawers, and I quickly find that she has taken some of her clothes. Her bag is missing, too, and it's clear that she has headed off into the night with the intention of not coming back for a while. I race back down the stairs and out of the cottage, and then I stop in the lane as I realize that I have no idea which way she might have gone. She has no family around here and no real friends, she has no-one at all. There's the man she met in the forest, but I doubt she'd turn to him when she knows she was wrong to see him in the first place, so I can only assume that she has struck off alone.

Finally, realizing that I have to start somewhere, I hurry along the lane and make my way out of the village, stumbling slightly as I head toward the pitch-black forest.

By the time I reach the tree-line, my sense of panic has multiplied massively and I keep imagining the worst possible things happening to her out here.

"Elizabeth!" I scream, cupping my hands around my mouth. "Come back!"

I bump against a tree. It's so dark here, I can barely see a thing. Elizabeth could be ten feet away and I might not spot her, so I stop and listen.

All I hear is a faint rustle of the wind in the leave high above.

"Elizabeth!" I shout again. "You have to come home!"

I stumble on, bumping against another tree every few seconds desperately trying to find my way through the forest. I'm already lost, and I can only pray that the Lord will help me find my daughter in her hour of need.

"What are you doing, Judith?" Shaltak's

voice asks in my head.

"This is your fault!" I snap.

"Is it? You're her mother, Judith. At the end of the day, isn't it *your* fault that she's in this mess?"

"I'm going to find her and bring her home," I reply, before bumping against another tree and then hurrying forward into the darkness. "She's a good strong, smart girl. I just need to find her."

"If she's strong and smart," Shaltak replies, "maybe she's better off without you."

"Of course she isn't," I reply, "she's -"

And then I stop in my tracks, shivering in the cold, as I realize that perhaps Shaltak is right. I think back to that day in the forest when I committed an unspeakable act, when I savaged my darling daughter, and I realize that I cannot be sure something like that would not happen again. While I have this demon in my soul, perhaps it *is* better that Elizabeth is away from me. I worry about her being lost and alone in the world, but she is resourceful and I am quickly able to convince myself that she will be able to get by. Yes, there will be dangers, but at least she will not be around me for a while. Perhaps I, ultimately, am the greatest danger of all.

Standing all alone in the darkness, I feel tears running down my face as I realize that – for now – I must let her go.

CHAPTER SEVENTEEN

"MS. PRENDERGAST," FATHER PERKINS says sternly, standing in the doorway, "I am sorry, but I am going to have to ask you to leave this place and to never return."

As I look out the window at the cold light of dawn, I can just about see Father Perkins' reflection in the glass. I hesitate for a moment, before turning to see that there is genuine fear in his eyes. And then, just as I am about to tell him that we can move past what happened, I see that he is holding a crucifix in his right hand, as if he intends to use it as protection against me.

I take a step toward him.

He immediately raises the crucifix.

"Are you scared of me?" I ask.

"I am scared of what you have become," he

replies, his voice trembling slightly with fear. "You were a good woman when I first met you, Judith, but something changed. I'm almost afraid to know exactly how this evil took root in your heart, but I have seen its face and I am in no doubt that it is real."

"And what do you think *it* is?" I ask.

"I do not want to say. Not here. Not now."

"I need your help," I tell him. "I know that I have this demon in my soul, and I can't get it out. I have allowed myself to become corrupted, Father Perkins. I never intended for any of this to happen. Inch by inch, every decision that I took was supposed to be for the common good. Yet somehow I didn't notice, until it was too late, that I had invited pure evil into my heart." I take another step toward him. "Please, you must know how to -"

"Stop!" he shouts, raising the crucifix a little higher.

"You must know how to end this," I continue. "I am not a bad person, I don't want this evil to dwell in my body, but I have no idea how to cast it out. If faith alone were enough, the demon would surely be gone by now. If prayers could drive it out, then I would have worn my knees to the bone." There are tears in my eyes now, and I know that Father Perkins is the only person who can help me. "The situation cannot be hopeless. I know there is a way to save me."

"I fear that the day has already been and gone," he says, with the crucifix still raised. "If you had come to me sooner, Judith, perhaps there might have been something I could have done. But this thing has taken hold of you and I know of no means now by which it can be removed."

"What would you have me do, then?" I ask, taking another step toward him. "Should I put a noose around my neck and hang myself? Should I cut my wrists? Would either of those sins be enough to cleanse my soul of this demon?"

"I can't help you, Judith," he replies. "May the Lord forgive me, but I am merely a priest. I have no experience with this kind of possession."

"Then help me find someone who *does* have the experience," I continue. "Please, before it's too -"

Suddenly a great pain erupts in my chest. I step forward and then I fall, dropping to my knees as I feel fire burning the back of my throat. I try to cry out, to beg Father Perkins for help, but I can't get any words out and – as I reach a hand toward him – I feel blood bubbling in my chest.

"I can't help you," he says, backing out into the corridor. "I know this means that I have failed. I'm leaving Briarwych, and I'm going to go and fight. I should have gone sooner. At least in the army, I can perhaps do some good. I completed my basic training some time ago and I imagine I shall be sent out to France or Belgium almost immediately. I'm sorry, Judith. I should have noticed sooner that something was wrong with you, but only the Lord can save you now. I shall pray for you, but truly... I fear that there is no hope at all."

"Please," I gurgle, as blood runs from my mouth and dribbles down my chin, "I need you, I..."

The pain in my throat becomes stronger, as if something is trying to force its way out.

"I need you, priest," another voice snarls, a voice filled with anger and hatred. "Why don't you come over here, so I can show you just how much?"

Turning, he hurries from view. I try to go after him but I fall forward and land hard on my elbows, then I somehow scramble to my feet and rush out into the corridor. I'm just in time to see the main door slam shut, and then a moment later I hear a key turning in the lock. Father Perkins is locking me in here, and I can only assume that he is worried about me escaping and causing trouble in the village. I stumble toward the door, still bleeding heavily from the mouth, and then I try the door handle, only to confirm that it is indeed locked.

"Do you think this will be enough?" the voice growls through my mouth, as I start clawing at the door. "I'm going to burn the people of this fucking village one by one! Do you think you can stop me by locking me inside this shitty little church?"

"May the Lord have mercy on our souls," Father Perkins says on the other side of the door. "I beseech thee, Lord, to see this evil and to cast it from our midst."

With that, his footsteps hurry away, leaving me to drop to my knees as waves of sobs burst through my body.

"Don't go," I whimper, with tears streaming down my face. "I can fight this, but I can't do it alone. She's too powerful."

But he's gone.

Sobbing on the floor, I realize that Father Perkins has left me. I reach up and try the handle again, forlornly hoping that perhaps a miracle has occurred, but the door remains locked and I am alone here in the church. Or rather, I am *not* alone, for I know that this thing is within my body and I know that it is gaining strength with each and every passing second. For now I am able to keep it back, but I fear that soon I shall be possessed entirely. Evidently the demon Shaltak wants to take control of my body so that it can walk out of the church and cause carnage in the world. In that case, there is really only one way in which I can stop the beast. I hesitate for a moment as I contemplate the awful deed that I must now commit, the sin that is my only hope.

"Elizabeth," I whisper, as I realize that I shall never see her again.

Closing my eyes, I imagine her having already found help. She is charming and kind and beautiful and intelligent, and I am certain she will be taken in by somebody. There are decent people out there in the world, and the Lord will look after my Elizabeth. In time, she might even come to understand that I loved her to the end.

Filled with the realization that I must get this over with, I scramble to my feet and hurry to the stairs.

"*Now* where are you going?" Shaltak asks. "I'm enjoying your panic, Judith, but time is pressing. I've learned a lot from you but I think it's time to experience more. I want to hurry things along. I want to get out there. I'm hungry for the world!"

I start rushing up the stairs, although in my haste I stumble several times. By the time I reach the next floor and make my way to the second set of stairs. I need to get up to the bell-tower before fear makes me change my mind.

"Poor little Judith," Shaltak laughs. "Did your boyfriend say mean things about you? You really thought that he'd marry you one day, didn't you?"

Finally reaching the bell-tower, I stop for a moment in the doorway as soon as I spot the open archway. I can feel myself starting to fill with doubt, but I also know that I have to stop Shaltak.

I reach into my pocket and take out the small crucifix that I first saw on that day with Prue. I hesitate for a moment, before closing my fist and holding the crucifix tight, in the hope that in some manner it might grant me strength.

"Forgive me," I whisper, "but this is the only way."

Rushing forward, I throw myself out of the tower. I see the ground far below, but at the last second my right hand reaches out and grabs the side of the arch, holding me in place, and then I'm pulled back until I slam down against the bell-tower's wooden floor.

"Judith, I'm impressed," Shaltak says. "I never thought you'd have the guts to do something like that."

I rush back to my feet and throw myself once more at the opening. Again, however, Shaltak forces my body to hit the arch and I instead fall back. This time my right hand slips open and the crucifix falls out of the tower.

"I just want this to end!" I sob, as tears run down my face. "I can't live like this!"

"I'm afraid I can't let you do this," Shaltak says. "I need your body."

Shivering with fear, I start to once again haul myself up from the floor. I turn to look at the arch, and I tell myself that this should be easy. All I have to do is throw myself through the gap, and then this madness will be over. I don't know what'll happen to Shaltak, but at least the threat to Briarwych should be ended. I just need to find the strength to push past Shaltak's efforts, so I take a moment to catch my breath and then I clench my fists. I can do this. I *will* do this.

"I love you, Elizabeth," I whisper, with tears in my eyes. "Dear Lord, help Elizabeth to understand everything. And keep her safe."

With that, I run at the arch and throw myself through harder than ever. I feel my feet leave the stonework, and for a moment it's as if I'm suspended in the air. Then, with shocking ferocity, something drags me back into the bell-tower. Reaching out, I grab the side of the archway and hold myself here, teetering on the very edge. I can feel Shaltak still trying to pull me inside, but I just need to move a few inches forward and then I'll fall. A cold wind is blowing against me, ruffling my hair, and when I look down I see the hard ground far below.

I can do this.

"Stop misbehaving," Shaltak says firmly. "You're starting to irritate me, Judith."

"I never wanted any of this," I whimper, as I try once more to find the strength that I'll need. "I will not allow evil to prosper in this world."

I try to step forward, but Shaltak pulls me back with more force. My fingertips are clinging to the stone wall, but I can feel the tips starting to bend as Shaltak tries to drag me inside. She's so strong, and I have to keep telling myself that I can force my way out. All I need is one moment of strength, one moment in which I'm able to overpower this monster. One moment in which I'm strong enough to save everyone from a demon.

"Be a good girl," Shaltak sneers, "and do what you're told."

"In the name of all that's holy," I reply through gritted teeth, "you can go to Hell."

Finally I throw myself forward. For a fraction of a second I feel as if I'm about to fall, but then Shaltak forces me back and sends me slamming back across the room. I scream as I land, and then my head hits a wooden edge and I feel a sharp pain crack through my skull. Everything goes black, and then for a few seconds there's nothing. I feel the weight of my body as it slumps against the floorboards, and then even the weight is gone. For a moment there's nothing, and it takes a few seconds before I'm even aware of myself again.

Groaning, I sit up and look toward the archway. I don't hear Shaltak's voice right now, but I can feel her presence still rippling inside my body.

I have to do this.

Stumbling to my feet, I'm shocked to find that I feel dizzy. I take a couple of faltering steps toward the archway and then I have to stop and lean against the wall. Then, with the last of my strength, I step up onto the ledge and begin to lean forward, only to find that I cannot.

I try again, but I am being held back. This time, however, the force is very different. This time, it's as if something *outside* the church is holding me in place. Shaltak must have found some other way of trapping me, and I feel a rush of panic as I realize that I might have missed my chance to get out.

"No!" Shaltak sneers suddenly. "I swear..."

Suddenly she screams. Clutching my hands against my ears, I try to block the sound out, but her scream is ripping through my mind with such immense power that I can barely even hear my own thoughts. I stumble away from the window and finally I drop to my knees, and at that moment the scream – which already seemed to be as loud as any scream could ever be – becomes louder still, threatening to crack my skull open. I cry out, wailing in agony as I wait for the sound to end, but it's getting louder and louder with each passing second. It's as if Shaltak is consumed with rage.

And then it stops.

Letting out a pained gasp, I fall forward onto my elbows. I wait, terrified in case the scream returns, but after a few seconds I realize that I can instead feel a slow, rumbling anger in the back of my mind. I raise my face slightly and look across the bell-tower, and then to my surprise I note that there is a shape slumped on the floor just a few feet away.

I stare for a moment, before tilting my head.

There is somebody else up here.

Getting to my feet, I stare down at the collapsed figure and see that there is blood pooling beneath its head. My vision is a little blurry but, as I take a step forward, I realize that the figure is wearing a dress that seems rather familiar. Indeed, the figure is wearing the same dress that I wear now, and its hair is in the same style, and...

Suddenly I let out a horrified gasp as I see a pair of dead eyes.

The figure is in the exact spot in which I fell just a moment ago, and somehow I seem to be looking down at a facsimile of myself. Slowly, cautiously, I kneel to take a closer look, and then I reach out and place a hand on the figure's shoulder. I do not understand what can have happened, but it is as if somebody has made a second version of me and has placed it here as part of some cruel and unusual joke. Yet that explanation itself does not make any sense, and as I stare at the dead face I cannot help but remember the moment when I felt my own head crack against the wooden step.

“Judith,” Shaltak's voice says slowly, “I'm very disappointed in you.”

“What is this?” I whisper, as a slow sense of dread begins to rise through my chest.

"Why did you fight me?" Shaltak continues, and I can hear the anger starting to rumble in her voice. "Look at your body! You've ruined the vessel I was going to take out into the world, and now..."

I continue to stare at the dead face, unable to avert my gaze.

"And now I am intertwined with you," Shaltak growls. "I was part of you when you died, and now somehow we are fused together."

Before I can respond, I feel an immense tearing sensation in my chest. I try to pull away, but for a few seconds it is as if part of my soul is attempting to rip itself free. Looking down at my hands, I worry for a moment that my vision has become blurred, but then I realize that it is my hand itself – indeed, my entire body – that seems to be rippling and doubling as if two versions are fighting for supremacy.

"You have no idea what a mistake you've made," Shaltak stammers, sounding a little panicked now as the sensation fades. "I'll find a way to cut this tie with you, Judith Prendergast. And when I do, you're assured of the slowest, most agonizing death that's possible. I won't stay trapped here with you for long."

I open my mouth to reply, but then I once again spot the dead body on the floor.

"How does it feel?" Shaltak asks. "You *know* you're dead, don't you? You're a pathetic imbecile, Judith, but even you must understand by now that you died in your struggle with me. I suppose it's partly my fault, though. I forgot just how fragile your worthless forms can be."

Still staring at the body, I slowly shake my head.

"What a pitiful death," Shaltak continues. "Do you think anyone cares? Do you think that even your dear daughter will give a damn now that you're gone? The whole village will probably have a party to celebrate. That's if they notice at all. Maybe they'll just get on with their lives."

"No," I whisper, "you're wrong. I'm not dead. I *can't* be dead. If I were dead, I wouldn't be here."

"You're trapped here forever, you stupid bitch," Shaltak replies. "Some souls fade into the ether after death. Others cling to certain places in the world. And now, thanks to your idiocy, I'm trapped here too. At least until I can figure out how to break away from you."

"No," I sob, as convulsions of horror start flooding my body. "Please, it can't be true."

And then, as I continue to stare at the corpse and as Shaltak's voice laughs in my head, I start screaming.

CHAPTER EIGHTEEN

Several weeks later

"DEAR LORD, I BEG you to hear me," I whisper, kneeling before the altar in the cold, empty church. "I have been your humble servant but I have erred. I have sinned and I have brought great suffering into this world and I beg for your -"

Suddenly there's a bumping sound somewhere nearby, and I flinch.

With my eyes still closed and my head still bowed, and with my hands still clutched together, I wait as silence returns. I don't know how long I have spent on my knees in prayer, but it must be many days now. I don't understand what is happening to me. I know only that the Lord will find a way to help me. I just have to show, first, that my repentance is real.

"I beg for your help," I continue, "not for my own benefit, but for the benefit of others. If my soul must burn in Hell, then that is right and proper. But help the others, Lord. Please, there is a demon among us and it must be stopped."

I wait, hopeful that this time I have finally been heard.

"Bless you, my child," a voice says suddenly. "I shall help you immediately."

A shudder runs through my chest as I realize that this is Shaltak again, playing another of her tricks. I refuse to respond, to give her what she wants, but I have no way to push her away.

"What's wrong, Judith?" she continues. "Has the cat got your tongue?"

I shall not be fooled.

"God doesn't answer you," Shaltak says. "Nobody cares about you, nobody except me. Won't you miss me when I find a way to leave, Judith? You and I have been rattling around in this place for weeks now, with just one another for company. And you're not exactly the most interesting of companions. In fact, I'd go so far as to say that you're rather boring."

"Lord, hear me," I whisper. "I am not -"

Suddenly I hear more voices in the distance, and this time I turn and look along the aisle. I can hear children outside, and I realize after a moment that they must be in the cemetery. Then, telling myself that perhaps they are merely another trick used by Shaltak to fool me, I look back at the altar.

"That took a while," Shaltak says. "I was beginning to think that the people of this little village were never going to come anywhere near the church again."

The voices continue, and finally I get to my feet. There is still a part of me that worries I am being tricked, but somehow I feel increasingly certain that the voices are real. I start making my way along the aisle as I listen to the children heading around the side of the building. As I hurry out into the corridor, I feel as if I am drawn to the voices, as if – hearing sounds of the living after being alone for so long – I cannot help myself. Indeed, as I head through to Father Perkins' office and then to the window, I am filled with hope.

As soon as I stop at the window, I see that there are two young children playing outside in the grass. I recognize one of the children as the Lansley girl, I believe her name is Audrey; the other child, a boy, I am not sure I have seen before. The sight of them fills me with such hope, and I almost tap on the glass before – at the last moment – remembering that perhaps I should not. For a moment, I merely watch them as they go about their innocent business. I remember what it was like to be a child. I remember what it was like to be free of sin.

"They really don't care about you, do they?" Shaltak's voice says after a moment. "I mean all the people of the village. I mocked you before, but even I didn't quite believe that you'd be ignored and forgotten like this. The people of Briarwych possess a special degree of hatred, don't they? It seems they're happy to just forget all about you."

The Lansley girl laughs, and I instinctively smile at the sound.

"Are you jealous, Judith?" Shaltak asks. "Do you miss the feeling of blood pumping through your veins?"

She's right.

I'm not jealous, exactly, but I *do* miss the feeling of warmth. I miss the sensation of my heart beating in my chest. That's not something I ever noticed when I was alive, but I notice its absence now. I have no right to feel sorry for myself, but I would so dearly like to feel alive again.

Suddenly the Lansley girl turns and looks this way, and our gazes meet.

"Can she see you?" Shaltak asks as the girl stares at me. "Does she see a ghost at the window?"

Too scared to know what I should do, I simply stand here and wait. The Lansley girl stares at me for a moment longer, before grabbing her friend's arm and saying something to him. I don't hear her words, but the boy quickly looks this way and he too appears to see me. Then, as if terrified, the two children run away across the cemetery and disappear into the distance.

"I think we have an answer," Shaltak says. "They'll go home and tell their families that they saw the ghost of Judith Prendergast. How do you think their families will react?"

"No," I reply, "I -"

"You're horrifying, Judith," she continues. "You're the ghost of Briarwych Church. You haunt this place now. How does that feel? You're the horror of the village."

Panicking, I turn and hurry out of the room, and then I make my way along the aisle before dropping once more to my knees and clutching my hands together.

"That won't help you," Shaltak sneers, "you fucking pig."

"Dear Lord I am your faithful servant and I have sinned but I beg your forgiveness," I stammer, determined to keep trying. "Help me get rid of this foul demon."

As Shaltak laughs, I continue to pray. Deep in my heart, I know that the Lord will soon answer.

CHAPTER NINETEEN

Several weeks later

MY SOBS BREAK THE silence of the church. I can't help myself. I'm cowering on the floor, weeping in the corner of the church. I have my hands over my eyes, but that doesn't help when the evil is already in my mind.

"I've been thinking, Judith," Shaltak says, after several days away, "maybe -"

"Leave me!" I shriek. "Don't you dare even talk to me!"

"Well, that's not very friendly, is it?"

"I can't hear you!" I sob. "I refuse!"

"I want to try something," Shaltak replies. "An experiment, if you like. I have rested and I want to see whether we can perhaps, together, project ourselves beyond the church. If only for a short time."

"I don't want anything to do with you!" I snap.

"Tough. We're stuck together for now." She pauses. "I've been thinking about that lovely priest. What was his name again? Oh, that's right. Father Perkins."

"I can't hear you," I say again, shaking my head.

"That name hurts you, doesn't it? It tears at your heart. There are scratch-marks, Judith, on the inside of your soul."

"Father Perkins is far away," I whimper. "He escaped, at least."

"Do you think so? Or do you think that he still thinks of you from time to time?"

"I don't want to talk about this," I reply, struggling to stay strong. "He escaped from all of this."

"I've been practicing," Shaltak replies. "Testing whether I can reach out, and I think I can. I believe I have made Father Perkins see you on several occasions, all the way out there in the war-torn lands of mainland Europe."

"You're lying."

"I'll prove it to you. And this time you'll be there too."

"You're a liar!" I snap. "Demon's always

lie."

"Don't you *want* to see him again?" Shaltak asks, her voice purring through my mind. "Don't you want to touch him?"

"I'm not going to fall for your tricks."

"Let's go and see him," Shaltak continues. "Let's go and see your precious Father Perkins."

"No," I stammer, "please, I -"

Suddenly I feel the air become much warmer. Lowering my hands, I see that I'm now towering over a bed. There's a figure in the bed, trembling and shaking, and after a moment the figure turns and – in the low light of the room – I see the terrified, tortured face of poor Father Perkins.

"His soul is dying, don't you think?" Shaltak says. "He can't face the truth. Why does he fear us? Why doesn't he love us?"

"Don't hurt him," I whimper. "Please, please don't hurt him. Leave him alone. Hurt me, but let him go."

I hear Shaltak laughing in my head, and then I look down and see that my hand is reaching out toward Father Perkins' face. I try desperately to pull back, but it's as if my form is not my own and I can do nothing as my hand touches his cheek. The horror in his eyes is enough to make me want to scream, but I can already feel my fingertips reaching down toward his neck.

"No," I whisper, "I won't let you kill him."

"You have no choice," Shaltak's voice says in my mind. "I shall slowly tear his head off, and you shall have no choice but to watch. Decapitation has always been my favored way of killing. It's just such a brutal way to end a human life. And while you cannot stop me, you shall feel every moment through your hands. You shall feel his skin tearing, and his hot blood rushing out, and his body shaking violently as he dies. All that violence contained in your hands. I want to ensure that you feel it all."

"No!" I scream, and with all my strength I manage to pull back.

Suddenly my back presses against the cold wall of the church, and I find that I'm back on the floor. My hands are outstretched in front of me, shaking terribly, but there is now no sign of Father Perkins.

"Interesting," Shaltak says after a moment. "How did you do that?"

Staring at my hands, I can't help but think back to the horrified expression on Father Perkins' face. He looked like a truly broken man, like someone had finally let fear consume his soul. I wanted to speak to him, to tell him that this is all my fault, to beg for his forgiveness. Instead, I was unable to say anything until I finally managed to bring myself back here to the church.

"You are stronger than you look," Shaltak

says. “You should not have been able to stop me. Is your love for that priest so strong, so pure, that it momentarily gave you such vast strength?”

“Leave him alone,” I whimper. “I won't let you hurt him.”

“We shall see.”

Shivering in the cold air, I roll onto my side and begin sobbing uncontrollably. It's my fault that Father Perkins has become such a crushed man, and I know I shall not be able to stop Shaltak forever. Then again, what choice do I have? I *must* stop her, I must stay strong, or she'll surely carry out her terrible threat. For now she seems to have retreated, and I can sense that her voice is not currently in my mind. I don't know where she has gone, and I am certain that she will return, but at least for now I am spared her torment. And I am sure that while she is gone from my mind, Father Perkins at least is safe.

I sob for hours. I keep trying to think of something that I can do to escape this horror, but there is nothing. If I could end my pitiful existence, I would do just that, but I am already dead and I do not know how to extinguish what is left of me. I can only pray to the Lord, for hour after desperate hour, begging him to see my agony and my contrition. I know I am not worthy of being saved, but at least the Lord can help those who might yet be hurt by Shaltak. Father Perkins and Elizabeth and the others need to be protected, so I pray and I pray for divine intervention, all through the night and then through the morning too, as the windows lighten and a new day arrives.

And then, many hours after dawn, I feel my thoughts swell slightly, and I stiffen with fear as I realize that Shaltak has returned.

"Your strength fascinates me," she whispers. "How you stopped me last night, Judith, I do not understand. I have contemplated the matter for many hours. It seems that you are not as pathetic as you seemed. Is it possible that I have misjudged you?"

"Leave me alone," I whimper. "Dear Lord, save me from -"

Suddenly a great force whips me up from the floor and slams me against the church's wall, with such strength that I let out a gasp of shock. For a moment I am pinned in place, and then slowly the force starts pushing me higher and higher up the wall until I am almost at the ceiling. At the same time, my arms are forced out to my sides, compelling me to assume the position of Christ on the cross.

"Save me, Lord!" I scream. "Condemn my soul to Hell, but end this torture!"

"Nobody cares about your soul, Judith," Shaltak explains calmly. "Do you think the people of this village don't know that you're in here? They might tell themselves that you have left, but in the backs of their minds they must realize. Perhaps some of them even heard your scream a moment ago, but they do not care one iota. Don't you think that perhaps they share some of the blame for your unfortunate predicament?"

"I just want it to end!" I cry out. "Do what you want with me, but leave the others alone!"

"You remain defiant."

"He's a good man," I whimper, as I feel tears streaming down my face. "He doesn't deserve any of this."

"Your love for that priest drives you," Shaltak replies. "Bow down to me completely, Judith, and I might yet spare him."

"Dear Lord," I continue, as I look up toward the ceiling, "I ask your forgiveness. I am wretched, and I know I cannot atone for all the sins I have committed, but -"

Suddenly Shaltak starts laughing loudly.

"But I beg you to intervene for the sake of all the others who might yet be hurt by this foul monstrosity."

"Foul monstrosity?" Shaltak chuckles. "Oh, I like that. Please, go on."

"Don't let her hurt Father Perkins," I continue. "He has been a faithful servant of yours, and he deserves to be spared from the consequences of my terrible mistakes."

"Open your soul to me completely, Judith,"

Shaltak says, "and I shall spare the priest."

"Lord, you must -"

"He won't help you!" Shaltak snaps. "He doesn't even hear you! Only I can do anything for you, Judith. The sooner you turn your face from God and accept me, the sooner your loved ones can be spared."

"I will not abandon the Lord," I sob. "I refuse to be -"

Before I can finish, I'm flung from the wall and sent crashing across the church. I slam against the pews and cry out as I fall to the floor. There was no pain in the impact, only shock, but I am weeping and shaking as I get to my feet. I want desperately for this to end, and I know that there is only one way that I can ever escape the dreadful compact that I made with this demon.

Slowly, I get down onto my knees and begin once more to pray.

"Dear Lord," I stammer, barely able to get the words out, "I shall not lose my faith in you. No matter how I am tempted by this demon, I shall not again make the mistake that I made when first I heard her voice. Look deep into my soul, deeper than I myself can look, and you shall see that I speak the truth. I am your faithful servant, humble though lost, and I beseech you to end the madness that I have created."

Nearby, Shaltak is laughing.

"I do not hear her voice," I continue. "Not anymore."

"Is that so?" Shaltak chuckles.

"I cast her from my mind. With your help, Lord, I send her away."

"You don't know what you're talking about."

"I beg you, Lord."

"You don't even know where you are."

"Leave me alone!" I yell, turning to look over my shoulder. "Leave my -"

And then I freeze, as I find that once more I am no longer in the church. I am in a completely unfamiliar place, in a rather bare-looking room with wooden floorboards. There is a window over on the room's far side, looking out to a sky that appears completely white. I can hear voices outside, distant voices of men shouting at one another. For a moment, I can only stand in shock as I look around the room and try to work out exactly where I am. This place feels utterly foreign. I know I am certainly not in Briarwych, not anymore, and I fear I am not even in England. Then, hearing footsteps, I turn and look toward a wooden door, which almost immediately springs open.

"No," I whisper, as I see Father Perkins and another man coming up into the room, wearing military uniforms. "Why have I come to this place?"

"Look how he walks," Shaltak says as Father Perkins and the other man make their way cautiously around the room, as if they're checking for something. "It's different now, isn't it? He has the sloping gait of a man who has entirely given up. Does fear consume his every waking moment, do you think? Is *his* faith gone?"

"His faith could never be destroyed," I reply firmly. "He is a true man of the Lord."

"Are you sure of that?"

"His faith is greater than mine has ever been," I continue, and once again I feel tears running down my face.

"Are you *really* sure?"

"I am," I tell her. "With every fiber of my being."

"You have faith in him."

"I suppose I do, yes." I watch as Father Perkins heads over to another doorway, where he stops and then crouches down. In that moment, I see that a thin wire has been left crossing the doorway, just a few inches from the floor. "You might have destroyed my soul," I continue, "but David Perkins is too strong even for the likes of you."

"Found one," Father Perkins says, turning to the other man. "It's not even that well-hidden. Do they think we're complete idiots?"

"Looks simple enough," his comrade says, heading over to take a look at the wire. "Standard procedure?"

"I think so," Father Perkins replies, before pausing for a moment and then turning to look this way.

Our eyes meet.

"No," I whisper, as I realize that he can see me once more. "I refuse to let this happen."

"Say, Frank," Father Perkins continues, looking up at the other man, "I just realized, I left my cutters outside. Stupid of me, I know, but could I ask you to go and fetch them for me?"

"What are you talking about?" the man asks. "I saw you with your cutters just now."

"I'm telling you, I don't have them. Let's not waste any more time than's necessary, eh? I'm sure there are plenty more booby-traps in this street. Go and fetch the cutters, and we can get on with our job."

"But..."

"There are a lot of people depending on us, Frank. We can't let them down."

The man hesitates, before sighing and heading back over to the top of the stairs. When he gets there, however, he stops and looks back toward Father Perkins.

"I'm sure you had them with you," he says. "Can't you check again?"

"Believe me, I've checked," Father Perkins replies, briefly glancing at me before turning back to the man. “It's dashed foolish of me, but I suppose I've been a little distracted this morning. You know what it's like sometimes. Now hurry up and fetch them.”

“And you're sure you're okay?”

“Why wouldn't I be?”

“It's just...” The man pauses, before looking around the room. He doesn't look straight at me, not exactly. It's as if he senses my presence but doesn't quite see me. “I woke up in the night,” he continues, turning back to Father Perkins, “and I happened to look over at your bed, Davey. Now, maybe I'm losing my mind, but for a moment there in the dark, I thought I saw...”

His voice trails off.

“You thought you saw what, Frank?” Father Perkins asks.

“This is going to sound stupid,” he continues, “but I remember you telling me about -”

“I wouldn't worry,” Father Perkins says suddenly, interrupting him. “Like you mentioned, we're all going a bit crazy out here. Trust me, as a priest in my civilian life I get a lot of people coming to me with their problems, and I hear it all. The best thing is to keep it inside. The more you talk about it, the more real it can seem, and then you're trapped in a vicious circle. I once knew a...”

He pauses for a moment.

“I once knew a good woman,” he continues,

"who let her fears overwhelm her. I don't think she knew how good she was, not really. She got battered down by some judgmental people who lived in the same village. And I still don't understand exactly how she became what she became, but I rather think that part of the problem was that she let the fears become too real. So really, Frank, I'd say it's best to keep it all inside and focus on what *is* real. Otherwise, even the very best of us can be destroyed. Even the very best of women."

"He loves me," I whisper, as I feel a sudden surge of hope in my heart. "He's defending me. He knows I'm not a monster."

"You might be right," the man says with a sigh. "I don't want to end up in the loony bin, do I? I wish I'd got a new pair of cutters myself after I lost the last pair, though. Would've saved me this traipse. Back in a minute."

With that, he starts heading down the stairs, and he quickly disappears from view.

"I knew you'd understand," I sob, turning to Father Perkins and seeing that he's still crouched next to that wire, still watching me. "Can you hear me?" I continue, before stepping toward him. "Oh, I loved you for so long. I still do. I let myself become cruel and evil, I made the most despicable choices, but I was a good woman once, I swear. I still am, somewhere inside, but I let this *thing* into my heart and now I can't get it out. Father, can you help me?

Perhaps your faith will still be enough to end this nightmare."

He pauses, before reaching out and putting a hand on the wire.

"Father?" I stammer. "Can you help me?"

"I tried praying," he replies, "so many times. And do you know what? It didn't work. In the end, we're all alone. I look at the world now and I don't see any good in it at all. Only bad."

I take another step toward him.

Suddenly he pulls the wire. In the blink of an eye, an enormous explosion rips through the room. I scream as I see the doorway disintegrate, and somewhere in the heart of the inferno I spot Father Perkins' body being blasted into pieces. Everything seems to slow down for a moment, and I stare in wide-eyed horror at the chunks of flesh and bone that spin wildly through the air. A wall of heat hits me and I feel the air rushing all around, and the noise is utterly incredible, and I start to think that perhaps this terrible wall of destruction will never end. Finally, however, it *does* end, and I am left standing alone in a room that has had one wall and a part of its ceiling destroyed.

Where Father Perkins was crouched a moment ago, there is now nothing but a hole in the floorboards.

"Father?" I whisper, looking around as I hear panicked voices shouting outside. "Father

Perkins?"

I try to spot him, to find him somewhere in the madness, but he is gone. Hurrying across the room, I search desperately for some sign of his body, but then I look down at my hand and I see that they are covered in blood. Then, turning, I catch sight of my reflection in a broken piece of glass, and I see that there is blood all across my face. In that instant, realizing that Father Perkins is gone, I scream.

Shaltak laughs, and I turn to find that I am back in the church, standing all alone halfway along the aisle. I look at my hand again and see that the blood is gone and my skin is once again deathly pale.

"What a pathetic display," Shaltak sneers. "You could have saved him, you know. You could have given your soul to me completely, Judith, and I'd have let him survive. Instead you were too proud. That's a real theme with you, isn't it? You valued your so-called faith above all else, you put your trust in the Lord and begged him to help you. And how did that work out?"

I pause for a moment, before realizing that Father Perkins is dead. Horrified, I sink to my knees and put my face in my hands, and I start sobbing wildly.

"He's dead because of you," Shaltak says, her voice rising above the sound of my own wailing sorrow. "You ruined a good man."

I cannot answer her accusation. Instead, overcome by sorrow, I let out the most anguished howl of pain. Until this moment I was always able to summon some words, to declare my faith, but now I am broken. Leaning forward, I arch my shaking back and try to rest on my elbows, only to slump down with my face against the cold stone floor as I cry out. All faith is gone, and all hope. What is left is only the realization that I failed, and that this demon has consumed me entirely.

A moment later, hearing a distinct clicking sound in the distance, I somehow manage to sit back up. I hear the sound of the church's wooden door being pressed quietly shut, and then I realize that there are footsteps out in the corridor. And then, to my horror, I see a familiar figure stepping into the arched doorway.

"Elizabeth," I whisper. "No..."

"Mother?" she calls out, looking all around as if she doesn't see me. "Are you here?"

"No!" I scream, stumbling to my feet and rushing over to her. I try to grab her by the arm and force her back out of the church, but somehow I am unable to touch her and I instead stumble and bump against the corridor's far wall.

"Mother, if you're here, give me a sign," she says, stepping through the doorway and then stopping to look toward the altar. "I know this is foolish," she continues, "but somehow... I know that you're here. You *are*, aren't you? I came back. Mother, I'm so sorry I ran from you. I came back for you, though. I realized that you need help. What you did to me in the forest, that wasn't really you. You'd never do something like that. I'm not scared anymore. I've come to help you."

"Such a pretty child," Shaltak whispers. "After everything you've done to her, she still loves you."

"Leave her alone," I stammer, as I feel an icy dread spreading through my body. "I won't let -"

"You won't let *what*?" Shaltak asks, as Elizabeth starts walking along the aisle. "You won't let her follow the same path as Father David Perkins? You won't let her suffer the same fate?"

"Leave my daughter in peace," I reply, terrified in case Elizabeth might see me. "For the love of -"

"The Lord?" Shaltak snaps. "Go on, I dare you. Ask again for help from someone who has consistently ignored your every plea. I dare you, say that name again and see how I respond."

I open my mouth to pray, but I do not dare.

"You are innocent," Shaltak continues. "That is the truth, Judith. I have been too harsh on you. It is the people of Briarwych who are to blame. If they had supported you from the start, if they had been true believers, everything would have been fine and you would never have succumbed to my advances. Instead, their constant judgment broke you down piece by piece until you felt unworthy, until doubts spread through your body like cracks in stone."

"No, it is *my* fault," I reply, still watching Elizabeth as she approaches the altar. "I know that now."

"Let me show you," Shaltak says, "how your life would have been if only the inhabitants of Briarwych had not ruined your life."

"No, I -"

Before I can finish, everything changes around me and I find myself back in my little cottage. Bright morning sunlight is streaming through the window, and the smell of egg and bacon is in the air. Startled, I look around, and I am shocked to see that Elizabeth is now sitting at the kitchen table, reading a book. I want to cry out to her, to tell her to run, but then she turns to me and smiles.

"Are you okay, Mummy?" she asks. "Why, you have a rather worried look on your face. You haven't burned breakfast, have you?"

"Elizabeth..."

"I suppose no-one's perfect," she continues, "not even you."

I open my mouth to tell her that she must get out of here, but then I hear footsteps on the stairs, and I turn just in time to see Father Perkins coming into the kitchen. And then, before I have time to react, he comes over and kisses me on the cheek, while placing a hand on my waist.

"Looking as beautiful as ever, my dear," he says with a chuckle. "I wish I could be with you at the meeting today, but you know how it is, church duties call. I hope you can knock some sense into the heads of the floral committee, though. Mrs. Wallingthorpe in particular seems rather stubborn."

"Father Perkins," I stammer, "I..."

"Father Perkins?" He plucks a rasher of bacon from the pan and starts nibbling the end. "You haven't called me that for a *long* time. I still remember the day I finally got you to call me David. That was when I knew we'd one day be married."

"Married?" I reply, tilting my head slightly.

"Mummy's in a funny mood today," Elizabeth says. "I don't know what's up with her, but I suppose it must be the stress of the flower committee. Old Mrs. Wallingthorpe can be a dreadful old -"

"Let's have none of that," Father Perkins tells her. "I won't have any step-daughter of mine speaking ill of people who are merely... I suppose we can call Mrs. Wallingthorpe misguided. But she's a good person, at heart."

"Mummy, are you sure you don't want to

have a sit down?" Elizabeth asks. "You really are looking *very* pale."

"Yes, darling, take a seat," Father Perkins says as he pulls a chair over from the table. "Lizzy's right, you do seem rather out of sorts."

He's right, I *am* feeling rather faint. And as I take a seat, I begin to realize that I might have been letting things get on top of me. Life can sometimes feel like an endless torrent of pressures and demands, and one can struggle from time to time to remain strong. Perhaps I have been a little harsh on myself of late, and I might be wise to slow down a little. After all, Elizabeth and Father Perkins need me so very much. They rely upon me.

"I had the most awful dream," I say finally, as Father Perkins – no, as *David* – kneels next to me, and as Elizabeth listens intently. "Everything was wrong. The world was all topsy-turvy and upside-down, and David... We weren't together."

"That sounds like a nightmare, darling," he says, reaching out and ruffling the hair on the side of my head. "But that's all it was. You know that, don't you?"

"I do," I reply, feeling a rush of relief in my chest. "Oh, David, I do realize that. It was terrible, but you're right, it *was* just a nightmare and it's over now. None of it actually happened, and we're all safe here at home, aren't we?"

"Of course, darling."

"And the church is alright?"

"The church?" He furrows his brow. "Of course the church is alright. Why wouldn't it be?"

Overcome with a sense of pure joy, I lean forward and put my arms around him, hugging him tight. There are tears in my eyes, and for a moment I can't help but think back to that awful nightmare about Shaltak and about everything going wrong. It all seemed so real, so real that I felt every second, but now it's over and I shall never ever take my life here for granted. I have learned the most valuable of all lessons, and I shall certainly give thanks to the Lord later for the fact that I have been saved from that dreadful dream.

"I love you," I sob, still clutching David tight, still scared to ever let him go again. "You have no idea how much I love you."

"And I love you too, darling. You know that, don't you?"

"Mummy, you're so funny sometimes," Elizabeth says. "You're really being quite silly today."

"And I love *you*," I say, turning to her. "I shall never -"

Suddenly the warmth of David's body is gone, and I find myself standing back in the church and staring along the aisle as Elizabeth stands alone the altar. The air all around me is so very cold.

"Wouldn't it have been nice?" Shaltak asks,

as fresh tears reach my eyes. "Oh, if only the people of Briarwych hadn't ruined your life."

"I want to wake up," I reply, as I realize that I must have slipped back once again into that awful nightmare. "I don't want to be here anymore. I want to wake up!"

Shaltak starts laughing.

"I want to wake up!" I scream, rushing forward before tripping and falling, and landing hard on my knees. "I want to wake up," I sob. "I don't want this to be my life."

"Mother?"

I look along the aisle again, and I see that Elizabeth seems to be staring straight at me.

"Are you going to make the same mistake again?" Shaltak asks. "Think of the look in Father Perkins' eyes as he died. Do you want to see the same look in your daughter's eyes when *she* dies?"

"No," I whisper, as Elizabeth starts making her way slowly along the aisle. "No no no no no, no, no no no..."

"Mother, I know you're dead," Elizabeth says as she gets closer. "I also knew, somehow, that I'd find you here."

"No no no," I stammer, getting to my feet, "no, no no no, no..."

"Mother, what happened?" she asks, as tears run down her cheeks. "I don't understand, Mother. Why did you die?"

"You know why," Shaltak says. "It was all *their* fault. Let me into the last holdout in your heart, Judith. You know I speak the truth. They need to pay for their constant cruelty."

"It was all their fault," I whisper, before realizing that I can feel a surge of anger and hatred rising through my chest. "It *was* all their fault."

She's right.

I would never have done that awful thing to Elizabeth without Shaltak in my mind, and Shaltak would never have been there if I had been stronger, and I would have been stronger if I had not endured a lifetime of shame and ridicule from the idiots in Briarwych.

"It was their fault," I whisper again.

"What do you mean?" Elizabeth asks, stopping in front of me. She pauses, before reaching out a hand and touching my shoulder. "You're a ghost, aren't you?" she continues. "But I can touch you. You're so cold, Mother, and you look so pale. Are you really dead? Is your body really up in the... I mean, is this all true?" Her eyes are filled with tears now, and she takes a step back as she stares at me with an expression of utter horror. "Mother, tell me it's not so. I just..."

She pauses, and then suddenly she slumps down and lands hard against the floor.

"Elizabeth!"

Rushing forward, I realize she must have

fainted with shock at seeing me. I gather her up into my arms and then I manage to get her onto one of the pews. Putting an arm around her, I hold her tight and kiss the top of her head.

"Listen to me very carefully," Shaltak says, "if you want your daughter to live."

"I do," I sob. "I'll do anything."

"When she wakes, you must make her your agent in the world. I was able to take us to visit Father Perkins, but that effort took a lot out of me and I must rest for a while. So you must use your daughter. Do you understand? I want you to prove your loyalty to me, Judith, even in death. The people of Briarwych destroyed your life, they destroyed the life you *could* have had. They destroyed Father Perkins' life as well."

"Yes," I reply through gritted teeth, as I continue to hold Elizabeth tight. "They did."

"They must pay," Shaltak continues. "This church is shuttered and abandoned for now, but eventually it will re-open. You might have to wait a week, or a month, or a year, or ten years, but churches never stay closed for long. Eventually a new priest will arrive here, and you must be ready. When the day comes, you will need Elizabeth to obey your every command. She's a strong, resourceful girl. The villagers of Briarwych might be reluctant to return to the church, but they *must* return, so that they can be punished."

"How?" I ask.

"I will let you know in good time. For now, you must simply ensure that Elizabeth is your obedient servant. Use her love for you. Make her obey you."

"I will," I reply. "I swear."

"And don't let me down," Shaltak adds. "Once I am assured of your loyalty, I shall know that I can use you for a greater purpose. But if you let me down, I shall take my anger out on your daughter. I shall snap the bitch's neck and rip her head off, and I shall throw her corpse to the depths of Hell so that she can be ravaged for all eternity. If you think she was violated with a rose, wait until you see what I can do with hell-hounds."

"No," I sob, holding Elizabeth tighter and tighter. "I'll do it. I'll prove myself to you. You're right, the people of Briarwych have to suffer, and I'll make sure that they do. I'll make them pay for everything they've done."

"Mother?"

Looking down, I see that Elizabeth's eyes are open, and that she's staring up at me.

"Who are you going to make pay?" she asks, her voice trembling with fear. "Mother, why do you look so angry?"

"I need you to do something for me," I tell her. "It will take time, but it's very important." I reach up and put a hand on the side of her face. I see her flinch slightly at my cold touch, but I know that I can trust her. "Elizabeth," I continue, "I need you to help me gain my revenge on the people of Briarwych."

CHAPTER TWENTY

I DO NOT KNOW how much time passes as I walk alone through the church. Sometimes I hear Shaltak's voice in my mind, reminding me of my purpose here. Other times I am left with only my thoughts, and with my memories of how happy I could have been. Sometimes I hear voices outside, and I stop at the window to look out; I see children playing in the cemetery from time to time, although they always run when they become aware of my presence. For a while, my loneliness feels as if it might be endless, and I have only my anger to keep me warm.

Occasionally Shaltak tries to pull the same trick as before. She tries to take us beyond the church, but at least this is one thing I am able to stop. I have found a way to concentrate my mind and hold us both here. She has tried to be sneaky, to catch me by surprise, so I have had to remain vigilant. It helps that I never need to sleep anymore, and that I am never hungry or thirsty. I am awake and sated all the time. This is a curse, but also in some ways a blessing. At least I am able to ensure that nobody else suffers the way Father Perkins suffered.

So I simply walk and I walk and I walk, and occasionally I have to stop for a moment and focus in order to keep Shaltak from projecting us beyond the church. Sometimes she rages and curses at me, but I take that as a sign that my efforts are working. And then, one day, after it feels as if an eternity has passed, I hear a sound I have not heard for many years.

I hear a key in a lock, fumbling slightly. I stop at the end of the corridor and wait, and finally I watch as the heavy wooden door slowly swings open.

This man is a priest. As soon as I see him standing there, silhouetted in the open doorway, I know that this is a man of the Lord. He is carrying a single suitcase, and he cuts a rather sad, lonely figure as he steps inside and places the suitcase on the floor. I do not dare move, lest I attract his attention, so at first I simply watch as he makes his way through the arched doorway. I can hear his footsteps moving along the aisle, and at the same time I feel a flicker of anger in my chest as I realize that finally, after all this time, Briarwych Church is going to re-open.

"See?" Shaltak whispers. "I told you. Churches never stay closed for very long."

***

Rain is crashing down and thunder rumbles in the sky high above, as the priest stands alone in the darkness and looks up toward the ceiling. It is several minutes now since he rose from his bed, and I rather think that he seems troubled by something. In the time since he arrived here, I have come to regard this new priest as a very calm, very ordered man. In ordinary circumstances, I would approve of him very much.

A humming sound begins to grow, above the sound of the dripping water and above the distant rumbles of thunder. I know that sound well, from the time I have spent here at the church. Bombers are heading out to France, which means that the war must still be raging. As soon as I think of the war, my mind returns to the horrific sight of Father Perkins in that room, and to the moment when he pulled on the wire and activated that German trap. I try to avoid thinking of such things, but now I feel myself getting overcome by emotion. By sorrow.

As the sound of the bombers fades, I turn and rush away, filled with panic. In the process, however, I inadvertently brush against the priest. I take several more paces before stopping, and then I turn to see that he is looking this way. He is not staring directly at me, but it is as if he sensed my touch. I wait, worried that he might somehow realize that I am here, and that he might then flee the church in a state of terror. He does no such thing, however. Instead, he continues to look around for a moment longer, and then he turns and heads back to the room in which he has been sleeping.

Where is Elizabeth? Everything is in place now. She must not let me down.

***

Morning sunlight streams through the window as I stand alone, staring out at the world. The glass is dirty and old, so I really can see no more than vague blurs of color. I can hear the rustle of nearby trees, however, and a moment later I realize I can also hear voices.

She is here.

"It's all rather a mess, actually," the priest says as he comes back inside. "Look down there, there's dirt on the floor. And here again, there seems to have been no work done for quite some time. So I'm afraid that the initial clean will have to be rather thorough. Somebody had even left a bicycle in here, so I don't think the place was really being used much as a kitchen back in the day."

Stepping out into the corridor, I freeze as soon as I see her.

Elizabeth – my dear, darling Elizabeth – is standing at the corridor's other end, and she is staring straight at me. I want to rush over, to hug her and tell her that I'm so glad she is finally here, but I manage to hold back.

"Is everything alright?" the priest asks, from the kitchen.

She turns to him.

"Oh, of course," she says, and then she goes through to join him. "Forgive me, I suppose I'm just surprised to be in here. I never thought..."

Her voice trails off for a moment.

"You never thought what?" the priest asks.

"Well, that I'd ever come in here again," she explains. "After Father Perkins left, and considering the circumstances, I rather thought that perhaps the church would remain locked forever."

I listen as they talk. Elizabeth is doing so well, she sounds completely innocent, perhaps even a little naive. I am impressed, and a little surprised, that she is able to lie so well. At the same time, I feel a growing sense of tension in my chest as I realize that the moment of truth is now fast approaching. Sooner rather than later, the people of

Briarwych shall return to the church, and then my plan for revenge can be put into action. Then I shall prove myself to Shaltak, and perhaps finally she will promise to never hurt my darling Elizabeth.

I know I should keep away from my dear girl and let her get on with things, but I have missed her so very much. Making my way along the corridor, I stop just outside the kitchen door.

"You are not the first person to get that look on their face while talking to me," the priest is saying. "Is there something about Briarwych Church that I should know?"

"Was she really not here?" Elizabeth asks.

"She? Who is *she*?" There is a pause. "There is only one key to this church," the priest continues, "and I can assure you that it is in my possession, and that it was given to me just a few days ago in London."

Good. He does not know of the secret spare key.

"Oh, I'm sure that's true," Elizabeth says, sounding rather convincing. "It's just that we all know what Father Perkins did when he left here a couple of years ago. Everyone knows. I mean, he... He locked her inside."

"I beg your pardon?"

"That was two years ago," she explains. "Several people saw the moment when he left, when he pulled the door shut and turned the key, locking Miss Prendergast inside."

I feel a shudder pass through my chest as I hear my dear Elizabeth refer to me by that name. At the same time, I am so very proud of her for fulfilling her role.

"She's doing well, isn't she?" Shaltak's voice whispers.

"She is," I reply, as Elizabeth continues to speak to the priest.

"Let's hope that she keeps it up," Shaltak continues. "You want your revenge, don't you?"

"Desperately," I tell her, although there is a part of me that feel a flicker of fear, for I know what must come next.

***

I stand completely still in the bell-tower, listening to the sound of somebody coming up the steps. I have been waiting here for a while now, anticipating the inevitable next stage of the plan, and I must admit that I feel no joy. Staring down at the floor, I cannot help but look at my poor, rotten body curled on the floor.

Finally the priest emerges from the stairwell. At first he doesn't notice my corpse at all. Instead, he looks up at the bells and then he glances around at the walls. He almost looks directly at me, but then he turns and I see the expression of shock on his face as he stops and stares at the dead body. For a few seconds, he simply stares and stares, as if he cannot believe what he is seeing.

"Father Loveford?" Elizabeth calls out from below. "Are you okay up there?"

He hesitates, before turning as we both hear footsteps on the stairs.

"Wait down there!" he says firmly.

"Is everything alright?"

"Wait down there," he says again, before stepping a little close to my corpse. "Whatever you do, do not come up here."

"Why?"

"Just do as I tell you," he says, making his way around one side of the body while I walk around the other. He clearly has no idea that I am here. "For the love of God, do not come up."

Even in death, even rotten and tattered, my face has a certain nobility. I remember the moment of my death so clearly, and it is strange indeed to see my features frozen in the form they took in those final seconds. I suppose there is still some dignity to this situation, and I know that my body – alone and abandoned as it has been – has nevertheless served a purpose. It has been useful. And while I suppose I might be a little biased, I truly believe that my corpse retains a degree of pride. Indeed, I have seen *living* people who are less dignified. Violet Durridge springs to mind.

Suddenly, hearing a whispering sound nearby, I turn and look at the priest. It takes a moment before I realize that he is uttering something under his breath. A prayer, perhaps.

"Is everything alright?" Elizabeth says as her footsteps resume on the stairs. "Father Loveford?"

"Wait!" he calls out. "Don't -"

Before he can finish, Elizabeth appears at the top of the stairs. She glances briefly at me, just for half a second or so, and then she looks down at my dead body. The expression of horror on her face is exquisite, and I am truly taken aback by her performance. Then again, perhaps she is merely channeling her genuine grief as she stares for a moment longer at the dead body. And then, with no warning, she breaks the silence with a scream.

Everything is going according to plan.

***

"I failed you," Elizabeth sobs, kneeling on the floor in the corridor, surrounded by the darkness and by the stench of the fire that was only just extinguished. "Mother, I'm so sorry. I love you so much, but I couldn't do it. I just couldn't burn all those people!"

"Wretched failure," Shaltak sneers, as if she's standing right behind me. "You know what you have to do. You can only redeem yourself by punishing her for her actions. And you can only punish her with death."

"She is the most beautiful, innocent girl in all the world," I reply, with tears in my eyes as I watch Elizabeth's anguish. "I should never have made her do this."

"Do you think you had a choice?" Shaltak asks. "Well, I suppose you did. And you chose to make the same mistake that led to Father Perkins' death. Now your daughter must die as well, and it *shall* be by your hands, even if I have to control your hands to make you do this."

"No," I whimper, "please, I'll do anything but you have to let her live!"

"Her fate is sealed," Shaltak replies. "The time of her death has arrived."

Before I can say anything, I suddenly spot a figure entering the church, and I recognize him at once. It is Father Loveford, a man I have come to respect over the past few weeks. He is a man of the Lord, and he has been good to my darling girl. Although everything feels doomed, I know that this man might yet be able to do something to help. It is far too late for me, of course, but Elizabeth must yet be saved.

"Lizzy," he says cautiously. "What are you doing here?"

"I'm so sorry, Mother," she whimpers.

"Lizzy," he says, taking a step toward her, "I

need you to look at me. Can you do that? Can you even hear me? Lizzy, can you -"

"Kill her!" Shaltak screams.

Elizabeth turns and looks at the priest, but at the same moment her body is pulled along the corridor until she slams into the floor at my feet.

"Do it now!" Shaltak roars. "Do it, or I shall do it for you with your own hands!"

"No!" I sob. "You can't make me!"

Sobbing wildly, Elizabeth looks up at me.

"I won't let this happen," I whimper, but then I feel my arms moving, and I see to my horror that Shaltak is using my hands to reach out to my daughter's shoulder. "I won't let you hurt her," I continue, trying desperately to stop Shaltak as she uses my hands to take hold of Elizabeth and twist her around until she has her back to me. "Don't you dare do this! You've hurt her so very much already."

"Lizzy," the priest says as he comes closer, "I -"

"She made me do it!" Elizabeth shouts at him, her voice filled with fear. "She made me, I didn't want to but she made me! She made me do it all!"

"A confession at the end," Shaltak sneers, as my hands tear the fabric at the back of her dress. "It won't save her soul."

"What, Lizzy?" the priest asks. "What did

she make you do?"

"I didn't want to," she cries. "You must believe me, Father Loveford! I didn't -"

Suddenly she stops, as Shaltak digs my fingertips deep into the skin on her back and starts carving a line through her flesh. Blood begins to run from the wounds, and I can feel the blood's heat against my fingers even as I try desperately to stop hurting her. I am cutting open the cuts that she caused with the cat o' nine tails, cuts that had begun to heal, and I am digging fresh marks too among the scars.

"If you'd just followed the plan," I whimper, "none of this would be happening. You brought this upon yourself."

"I didn't!" she sobs. "Stop saying that!"

"Shaltak might have let you go," I sob.

"Lizzy, you're imagining things," the priest says. "You're not -"

"I didn't want to do it!" she shouts, suddenly pulling away and slamming her head against the wall.

"Lizzy!" the priest calls out. "Stop!"

"I didn't want to do any of it!" she screams, as Shaltak forces me to grab her once more from behind. "She made me, Father Loveford. She made me do all those wicked, wicked things!"

"It wasn't me," I tell her, desperately hoping that she'll understand. "It was Shaltak!"

"Are you talking about your mother, Lizzy?" the priest asks. "You must have loved her very much. I can tell that, but your mother... I am sorry, but your mother is dead, and you cannot take it upon yourself to punish those you deem responsible. Only God can stand in judgment upon their souls, and you must trust that he will see their true natures when the time comes."

I let out an agonized whimper as Shaltak drives my fingertips deeper into Elizabeth's back. After a moment, I realize that she's carving her name into the flesh. I try desperately to stop her, but for a moment I am absolutely powerless.

"She's not yours!" I sob. "You can't have her!"

"You mustn't listen to the voice," the priest says as he steps closer. "The voice is in your head."

My fingertips are digging so deep now, and the nails are starting to scratch against her poor bones. Yet again, I am hurting my darling girl.

"Come to me," the priest says, reaching a hand out toward her. "Lizzy, ignore the voice in your head and come to me."

"Mother, I'm sorry," Elizabeth whimpers. "Forgive me."

"You have done nothing that needs to be forgiven," I tell her, as Shaltak continues to rip her back apart. "This is all my fault, my darling. It's all my fault, but I'm going to fix it."

"I shall pull her heart out and make you squeeze it," Shaltak sneers.

"It's over now," the priest says, stepping closer and closer to us. "I shall get you the help that you need. Do you understand? I'll help you, and -"

Suddenly he stops, and when I look at him I realize that he's staring down at my hands as Elizabeth's blood flows from her wound. It's as if, after all the time he has spent here at Briarwych Church, he finally sees me. I want to tell him that this isn't really me, that I would never hurt my poor dear girl, but Shaltak has taken control of my every move and I can only watch as my fingertips dig deeper and deeper into Elizabeth's back. I try to force Shaltak out of my mind, but if anything she's getting stronger.

"What is that?" the priest stammers.

"I'm so sorry," Lizzy cries, leaning a little toward him. "She made me do it. She made me do all of it."

Shaltak forces my hands to keep working, to dig deeper into her flesh. At the same time, no matter how hard I try to scream, I feel Shaltak forcing my face into a grimace of hatred. She is getting stronger by the second, and she has begun to take over my entire form.

"This is what happens," Shaltak whispers in my head, "when you and your little whore of a daughter disobey me. I really should have finished the little bitch off with that rose. I should have jammed it in so deep, until the end popped out through one of her eyes!"

"She made me kill the poor man at the airbase," Lizzy sobs, as my fingers dig deeper and deeper, "to silence him. She made me steal the petrol. She told me to wait, she said eventually everyone would come to church, and that then I'd be able to avenge her death, but... But I failed her. I was weak, I let them go. Don't you see now?"

I want to tell her that she's wrong, that I understand everything, but I can't get the words out. Shaltak has full control of my body now.

"Lizzy, come to me," the priest says. "Lizzy, hurry. Lizzy! Now! Lizzy, get away from her immediately! Lizzy! Now!"

"I'm sorry," she whimpers, as I feel Shaltak's strength growing and growing in my body, pushing my own soul aside until I am filled completely. "Father Loveford, I'm so, *so* sorry."

"If you -"

Suddenly I lunge at the priest, or rather Shaltak lunges at him in my body. He falls back and I land on top of him, and I scream as I grab his throat. His head bumped hard against the floor as he landed, and I think he might have knocked himself out. I desperately want to pull away, but instead my hands tighten around his neck.

"What a handsome head," Shaltak sneers in

my mind. "First, I'm going to rip it from his body. Then, since she has failed us so miserably, I shall kill that miserable girl. Perhaps I shall have her bash her own brains out against the wall. Or it might be more amusing to throw her from the bell-tower. Yes, that's how I'll kill her. You'll enjoy that, Judith, won't you?"

"Please don't do this," I whimper.

"You're not strong enough to stop me!" she snarls, tightening her grip again. "You're going to feel his blood as it -"

"No!" Elizabeth shouts suddenly, rushing at us and grabbing the priest, and trying to drag him away. "I won't let you hurt him, Mother! I love him, I won't let you do this!"

"It's not me," I manage to tell her. "It's Shaltak!"

"Who?" she asks.

"It's -"

Suddenly she gasps and takes a step back. At the same moment, I regain control of my hands and pull away from the priest.

"Run!" I shout at Elizabeth. "You must get out of here!"

She stares at me for a moment, and then slowly she tilts her head and begins to smile.

"Elizabeth, leave this place!" I cry. "You have done nothing wrong, but I cannot see you like this! Get away, before Shaltak -"

"Before Shaltak *what*?" she snaps back at me, with hatred in her eyes. "Before Shaltak takes control of my body and makes me leap from the bell-tower?"

"Before -"

Stopping suddenly, I realize that her grin is growing and growing, and after a moment she begins to laugh.

"Elizabeth, what are you doing?" I ask, still hoping against hope that my fears are unfounded. "Elizabeth, please, tell me that you're not -"

"That I'm not what, Mummy?" she giggles. "What's wrong? You look upset. Don't worry, the real Elizabeth Prendergast is deep in here, and she's screaming so loud. She wants to retake control of her body, but she doesn't stand a chance. I'll give it back to her soon, though. Just as soon as she's begun to fall. That way, you'll get to hear her real final scream as she plummets."

Suddenly she turns and runs, and I watch in horror as she races up the steps that lead high up into the church.

"No!" I gasp, as I suddenly realize what's about to happen. "Stop! You can't do this!"

Running past the unconscious Father Loveford, I hurry after Elizabeth, desperately trying to get to her before Shaltak can make her jump. I can hear her footsteps ahead, getting further and further away, and I run as fast as I can manage.

Finally I get all the way up into the bell-tower, just in time to see that Elizabeth is standing in one of the arched openings, silhouetted against the stars. She is standing as I once stood, when – long ago – I tried to destroy the evil that had taken root in my soul. This horror is in danger of repeating itself. And then, slowly, she turns and grins at me.

"Goodbye, Mother," she sneers. "Remember. This is all your fault."

With that, she turns and topples over the edge.

"No!" I scream, rushing forward.

In an instant, Elizabeth's body is pulled back into the bell-tower, until she's once against standing in the archway.

"Clever," she says with a grin. "You're a little more powerful than I'd anticipated, Judith, but it won't last. I know you humans tend to think that love conquers all, but that really isn't the case. Love is a weakness that leads fools and dreamers into terrible mistakes."

She starts to send Elizabeth falling forward again, but at the last moment something stops her.

"I will not let this happen," I say firmly, as I focus on the thought of keeping Elizabeth safe. I can tell that Shaltak is still trying to throw her from the tower, but at the same time I can feel myself pulling in the opposite direction, forcing Elizabeth to stay up here.

"Let her go," Shaltak sneers, still speaking through Elizabeth. "You might as well get it over with. She's screaming in here, Judith. She's terrified, her mind is breaking apart. You're only prolonging her agony, so let's just get this over with."

"No!" I sob, with tears streaming down my face. "I'll never let you do this!"

"You'll get tired soon," Shaltak replies. "Your mind isn't that powerful."

"Lizzy!" Father Loveford shouts suddenly as he emerges from the top of the stairs. "It's me. I need you to come away from the edge." He steps up behind her and starts to reach out toward her wrist. "Let me help you," he says. "Lizzy, things might seem bad now, but there's a way out of this. For a start, you needn't worry about what happened at the airbase. You have my solemn vow that I shall breathe not one word about any of this to Corporal Bolton. He'll never find out that you were responsible. Maybe that's wrong of me, but I won't let them get their hands on you. I just can't. They'd..."

He pauses for a moment.

More tears run down my cheeks as I struggle to hold Elizabeth in place. I can feel Shaltak still trying to push her over the edge, but somehow I'm managing to keep her right there on the ledge. I don't even know how I'm holding her back, but it's as if by concentrating I'm able to cancel out at least a small part of Shaltak's power. And as the priest gets closer to Elizabeth from behind, he too seems to be helping, as if between us we're slowly beginning to counter everything that Shaltak tries.

"Come down with me," he says, still almost touching her wrist.

"Fine," Shaltak says suddenly, returning to my mind. I gasp as I realize that she's left Elizabeth's body. "We'll do this the fun way."

Suddenly the priest turns and looks straight at me.

"You're not real," he says, as his eyes widen with fear. "You can't be real."

I want to tell him to run, to tell him that he must take Elizabeth with him, but I can't get the words out. Now that she's back in my body, Shaltak is once again far too powerful.

"You're not real!" the priest shouts again. "In the name of all that's holy, I know that you cannot be real!"

I feel myself stepping toward him, and I'm powerless to stop Shaltak using my body.

"Stay back!" he says firmly. "You will not come anywhere near her, do you hear? You will not take so much as one more step!"

"Time to give her a push," Shaltak whispers as I look up at Elizabeth. "Don't you want to hear her scream, Judith? At least for a few seconds, until she splatters all across the ground far below. I have to be honest with you, I haven't had this much fun in centuries."

"Lizzy, you must get down at once," the priest says as he tries to block my path. "Lizzy, do you hear? Climb down from that ledge!"

Shaltak forces me to take another step forward.

"Stop!" this brave priest says firmly. "In the name of the Lord, I command you to stop at once!"

Stopping, I look at Elizabeth for a moment longer before slowly turning and looking at the priest. I want to warn him, but I'm powerless to resist Shaltak's control of my body.

"You are an abomination," the priest continues, and he's right. "You are ungodly. Leave this house of the Lord and do not come back. Your transgression here is over. Flee, dark spirit, for you..."

His voice fades, as Shaltak smiles a smile with my lips.

"You are an abomination," he says again. "You are not right here. By that I mean that you desecrate the very ground upon which you stand and..."

He takes a deep breath.

"How dare you set foot in this church?" he continues. "You are -"

Suddenly Shaltak forces me to reach out and touch Elizabeth's back. I want to pull away, and I try with every last ounce of strength to resist, but I can feel my fingertips pressing against the bloodied marks that cover Elizabeth's back. The priest shouts at me, warning me to stop, but I can't fight Shaltak and slowly I push my darling daughter forward.

"Here comes the scream!" Shaltak sneers.

"No!" I scream, pulling back just as the priest turns and grabs Elizabeth's ankle.

For a moment, I feel a rush of panic, but then everything goes black and I slump down against the floor. I squeeze my eyes tight shut, waiting for Elizabeth's cry, and then after a few seconds I slowly open my eyes as I realize that somehow I'm back downstairs in the corridor on the church's ground floor. There has been no cry, no scream, and deep down I can tell that my daughter is still alive. I managed, at the very last moment, to hold Shaltak back, to prevent her from pushing Elizabeth quite as hard as she'd intended.

And now I can feel Shaltak's anger rising in my mind.

"How dare you defy me?" she sneers, sounding weaker than before. "How dare you and that priest stand in my way?"

"I *can* stop you," I manage to say through gritted teeth. "You're trapped here with me, aren't you? Otherwise you'd have left by now, but you must be trapped somehow. And it might be difficult, it might be almost impossible, but I can hold you back. At the very least, I can slow you down, and sometimes that might be enough." Getting to my feet, I start stumbling forward, hoping to reach the altar, but then my legs weaken and I almost fall. Stopping in front of the main door, I try to once again find the strength that – moments ago – let me stop Shaltak in the bell-tower. "I'm not defenseless against you!"

Suddenly I hear footsteps, and I turn to see that Father Loveford has carried Elizabeth down here. My girl looks to be unconscious, and after a moment I see from the expression on his face that the priest is able to see me. I want to cry out to him but Shaltak is holding me back, and I can feel her getting stronger again in my body, as if she's preparing to attack them once more.

"You're not real," the priest says as he carries Elizabeth toward me. "I know you're not."

"Don't fight this," Shaltak gasps in my mind, but I can tell that she's getting even weaker. For the first time, I'm managing to hold her back, but I don't know how much longer I can manage.

"You're not real," the priest continues as I look down at Elizabeth. "You're... I... you're..."

My poor girl.

Shaltak might be out of her body, but I can't imagine what damage she might have done while she was in her mind. Can Elizabeth recover from her brief possession, or is she doomed to never wake up? I can sense her soul, I can tell that she's in there somewhere, but something seems to be keeping her unconscious.

"You *are* real," the priest says suddenly. "How would I have known your face before I saw that photograph? You are real and..."

Slowly, I turn and look at him. He has the face of a kind and decent man, and it is clear that he loves Elizabeth very much. I want to tell him that I see all of this in him, and to tell him that I never wanted all of this to happen. To speak, however, would mean momentarily losing my focus on holding Shaltak back, and then she'd be able to attack them again. She's already getting stronger, and I can only hope that Elizabeth will be taken from this place before it's too late. Once she's out of the church, I believe Shaltak will be unable to reach her, at least if I am able to hold her back. For that to happen, though, this priest must get past me.

"You can't hurt her," he says suddenly. "Not now. If you could hurt her, you'd have done it by now. Maybe you can whisper in her ear and convince her to leap to her death, but you can't really *do* anything to her. Maybe you can scratch her back from time to time, but that's not enough for you, is it? Even that push in the bell-tower was more a hint than a proper push. Maybe the push was the absolute strongest move you could make and -"

Suddenly Shaltak bursts through and forces

me to lean forward, and I let out an angry snarl. I'm able to regain control, but I can feel Shaltak getting stronger and stronger.

"And that's all you can do!" the priest says as he takes a step back. "You can't even leave the church, can you? Otherwise you'd have wrought your revenge upon the villagers long ago. Mrs. Canton didn't actually see you from her window that night, it was just a guilt-induced vision. You're trapped here in the place of your death, and you'll be trapped here forever, which means I only have to get Lizzy away from you, which means..."

His voice trails off. Why doesn't he just leave? That's all I want. Shaltak is starting to break through and I don't know that I can hold her back for much longer.

"You *are* real," the priest says, "but that doesn't matter. Not once we're out of this place."

And then he does it. He steps forward, and I close my eyes as I feel him carry Elizabeth straight through me. In that instant, I sense her soul more strongly than ever, and I realize that she's definitely still in her body. At the same time, I can feel Shaltak screaming in my mind, flailing in a desperate attempt to leap back into Elizabeth. I'm ready for her, though, and I manage to hold her back with the very last of my strength. I'm shaking wildly, but I just have to stay strong for a few more seconds, and finally the priest passes through me and I realize that he's almost out of the church.

"You can't stop me!" Shaltak shouts in my head. "You're nothing!"

Suddenly my strength fails and I feel Shaltak rush back into my body. In that instant I turn and lunge at the priest, but to my relief I see that he and Elizabeth are beyond the threshold of the church. I fall toward them as Shaltak screams through my mouth, but as I cross the threshold I fall into an immense darkness. For a few seconds I feel nothing at all, and then I land on the cold stone floor and look up to see that I'm back in the corridor. I look toward the door and see that the priest is out there with Elizabeth still in his arms. Finally, just to make absolutely certain that Shaltak can't get to them, I reach out and force the door to slam shut.

Left alone on the floor, I realize that Elizabeth is safe. I shall never see her again, and she might never recover from the damage that Shaltak inflicted, but at least she has a chance.

I saved her.

"You have no idea what you've done," Shaltak sneers in my mind, still sounding a little weakened. "Do you think you've stopped me? All you've done is delay me and make me angry. And while I wait for somebody else to come into this church, I am going to greatly enjoy torturing you for your actions."

"Help!" I hear the priest shouting outside.

"Help us! Please, somebody help us!"

"I don't care," I reply, with a growing sense of absolute joy as tears of relief run down my face. "I deserve everything you do to me, but at least Elizabeth is away from this place. And I know that so long as she never returns to this church, you won't be able to harm her." In my mind's eye, I briefly relive that terrible moment with the rose and its thorns, but then I force myself to imagine Elizabeth safe out there in the world. Even if Shaltak tries again to reach out from the church, as she did when she tormented Father Perkins, I shall find the strength to keep her back. "She is safe," I say firmly, through gritted teeth. "Now and forever. And that is all that matters."

"Try to remember that," Shaltak growls, "as I torture you for decades."

CHAPTER TWENTY-ONE

Many years later

"MUMMY, PLEASE," ELIZABETH SOBS as worms continue to wriggle through holes in her face, "why are you doing this to me? Why did you -"

Suddenly she's gone, in the blink of an eye, and I'm left on my knees in the cold, dark church. I stare down at the floor, waiting for the next nightmare to begin. There's always a next nightmare. Shaltak torments me for days on end and then leaves me trembling in fear for a short while before launching another round of horror. Sometimes the gaps between nightmares last for weeks, other times for just a few seconds. There seems to be no end to the ways in which she manages to torture me.

And then, suddenly, I hear a very faint clicking sound and I look along the corridor. The main door remains locked as usual, although after a moment I realize that there's somebody out there, somebody who seems to be trying to get the door open.

“What did I tell you?” Shaltak's voice whispers in my ear. “Churches never stay shut. Somebody always comes along to open them.”

The sound stops, and a moment later I realize I can hear voices outside, as if some people are walking around the building. A moment later, getting to my feet, I start walking toward the door. I'm so dazed – so used to long stretches of boredom punctuated by brief, haunting nightmares – that I barely even remember how to think anymore. And then, as I get to the door and reach down to touch the lock, I realize that I'm allowing Shaltak to guide my body.

“No,” I whisper, pulling away, but the lock has already clicked and I can hear Shaltak laughing in my mind. She's been waiting for this moment, and it has finally arrived.

Feeling distinctly unsteady, I take several steps back. I don't know how long it has been since living people entered this church, but it must be at least several decades since Father Loveford took Elizabeth out of here. I feel a flicker of panic as I imagine Elizabeth out there now, but then I remember that Elizabeth would most likely be an elderly woman by now. Besides, I rather think that I would sense her, which means that the voices must come from new people. Sure enough, as the heavy door creaks open, I realize the voices sound young.

Suddenly a female figure comes into view and stops in the doorway, silhouetted against the cemetery.

I take several more steps back as I feel Shaltak's presence growing in my body. I have to remember how to hold her back, but at first I only feel her getting stronger.

"Come on," a young male voice says outside, as another set of footsteps comes toward the door, "let's -"

He falls silent for a moment, and then the female figure takes a step forward.

"Hey, stop!" the male voice calls out. "You can't seriously be going in there!"

When Elizabeth was here, I managed to find a way to hold Shaltak back, but right now I'm struggling to recall precisely how I achieved such a thing. Perhaps Elizabeth's plight gave me extra strength, but I have to find that strength again. I can feel Shaltak's hunger growing, and if she's been ravenously waiting all this time for the moment when these two youths enter the church. Whatever she plans to do, I know it will be terrible.

"Kerry, we have to go home now," the male voice continues. "We're not allowed to be in here. This is a really bad idea."

"So are you coming," the girl replies, "or are you an even bigger chicken than I thought?"

"Grow up," he says. "How did you even open this thing, anyway?"

"I won't let you do this," I whisper, clenching my fists as Shaltak gets stronger and stronger in my mind.

"It was open when I came back around," the girl continues.

"How did -"

"Obviously I did something when I was using the knife. I unlocked it without realizing, and then a gust of wind must have blown it open. Neat, huh? I've spent time on the streets, I know how to hustle."

They continue to argue as they come into the church. I stand completely still, focusing on the strength of Shaltak as she ripples through my body. Despite my every effort, I know that she's become stronger and bolder with every passing second, and after a moment I'm unable to stop myself walking forward along the corridor. I can hear the youths arguing in the old office, but to my relief I find that I instead walk through to the aisle and start making my way along the corridor. Shaltak has a plan, and as I move through the moonlight I try to once again summon the strength that I shall require if I am to stop her.

"I won't let you harm them," I say through gritted teeth. "I am not a -"

Suddenly an immense pain bursts through my mind, causing me to gasp and stumble. I drop to my knees, but I refuse to fall all the way down, and as I get back up I hear Shaltak's low, murmuring laugh starting to rise through my thoughts.

All around, the old pews are broken and burned. My heart weeps to see the devastation that has been caused to my once beautiful Briarwych Church.

"It's time to send a message," Shaltak says, as I make my way up to the altar, "to anybody who might be keeping an eye on this church. The miserable locals are of no use to me. If I know human nature at all, however, then there will be somebody out there, somebody far away perhaps, who will seek me out and try to make a deal."

"I refuse to let you hurt these people," I say firmly, as I hear the youths still arguing. "I will stop you."

"Not this time," she replies. "Your pathetic show of strength caught me by surprise last time, but that plan won't work again. Your daughter Elizabeth is dead, by the way. Did I mention that? She lived a life of agony, screaming in a cell, and eventually she scratched out her own eyes and beat her head to a pulp against a wall."

"No," I say, shaking my head, "that isn't true."

"She blamed you to the very end," she sneers. "She cursed your name."

"You're just trying to weaken me with lies," I reply, "but I see through your petty little games. I don't know what happened to Elizabeth after she left this church, but I know she strong." There are tears in my eyes now. "If she is dead now, then she is at peace. And I also know that you were unable to reach out and hurt her from here in the church. I was always able to hold you back."

"Whatever," Shaltak says. "Once I'm away from this place, and away from you, I can really have some fun."

"I won't allow that to happen," I tell her. "I shall ensure that you are trapped here with me forever."

"Echo!" a female voice suddenly shrieks.

I turn as the voice echoes in the air all around us, and I see that the girl is already almost here at the altar.

"Fuck!" she shouts, and her voice echoes again.

"Such crude young things," Shaltak whispers. "Come on, Judith, I know you. You must abhor this wretched child."

The youths are arguing again. I know that

Shaltak is still trying to weaken my resolve, which actually gives me strength since I take it as a sign that she is worried. If she felt that I could not hold her back, why would she bother with these constant attempts to make me lose heart? Stepping around the altar, I feel a flicker of panic as I realize that I might yet be unable to entirely hold Shaltak back, and then I turn and see that the girl has reached the end of the aisle. As she comes closer, she jumps up and sits on the altar, placing a bag next to her before shining some kind of light around. She is most disrespectful, but I refuse to let Shaltak manipulate my anger. She wants my anger to fuel her. Maybe she even *needs* my anger.

Suddenly the girl turns to me, and I see her eyes widen with shock.

She sees me!

Before I can stop her, Shaltak reaches out and grabs the left side of her face. I try to pull back, but her grip on the girl is already too strong.

“What are you doing here?” Shaltak screams through my mouth. “What do you want in my church?”

The girl tries to pull away, but she's helpless. I knew Shaltak was strong, but the sheer ferocity of her power has left me struggling to hold her back. I try desperately to stop Shaltak, but already she's twisting the girl's head around as if she means to detach it from her body.

"Why are you in my church?" Shaltak sneers, and this time her voice comes not only from my mouth but also from the mouth of the girl. "What do you want here?"

I can feel every ounce of the girl's fear. Her mind is screaming, but of course she's far too weak to resist Shaltak. That's my task, so I pull as hard as I can on the demon's mind and try to draw her back into my own head. I feel so utterly weak, however, and Shaltak keeps asking the same questions over and over again, still speaking simultaneously through both mouths. I can't imagine why she's doing any of this, or what she stands to gain, but her strength is burning too hot and too hard for me to restrain her.

"Why are you here?" Shaltak's voice asks, as the boy comes closer to the altar. "What are you doing here in my church?"

Squeezing my eyes tight shut, I try to find some last reserve of strength that I can use, but Shaltak is utterly overwhelming. I try to cry out, but my body is not even my own and I can hear Shaltak's voice still speaking, still asking those same questions no matter how hard I try to stop her. For a moment, I begin to feel that this misery shall never end, that Shaltak has finally been unleashed.

And then, with no warning, I feel my hand pull away from the girl. Opening my eyes, I step back and let out a shocked gasp, and I see the girl slithering off the altar.

"Hey, are you alright?" the boy asks her as he crouches down. "What the hell were you just on about there?"

Trembling with fear, I try to regather my composure. The boy is still talking to the girl, still trying to find out what happened. I hold my hands up and see that they're trembling, and I can still in some way feel Shaltak's power coursing through my body. Her strength was tremendous, and for the first time I worry that there is no way that I can ever hold her back. And if I can't hold her back then who will?

Hearing footsteps, I turn and see that the girl is running away.

"*Excuse* me?" the boy calls after her. "Seriously? I follow you into this creepy-ass church and I wait around for you in the freezing cold, and then *you* just take off on *me*?"

He peers at something the altar, and then he picks up a small device and shines its beam around the church. I want to warn him, to tell him that he must run, but I am too weak to utter a word. Instead, I simply watch as the boy's beam of light illuminates the ruined husk of this once-magnificent house of worship.

"Screw this," he says eventually, and then he starts to walk away. "I am so out of here."

Once he's gone, I remain completely still at

the altar. I don't understand what just happened, but I can feel Shaltak's rising sense of satisfaction. I had thought she meant to kill the girl right there and then, yet now it is clear that her intentions are rather different.

"The signal has been sent," she whispers in my head. "Now I must wait."

I don't know what she means, but I am afraid. For the first time in a while, she sounds confident again. And then, just as I am about to turn and walk away, I spot something glinting on the altar. I reach down, and to my shock I find the same silver crucifix that I dropped from the tower all those years ago. How it ended up back inside the church, right here on the altar, I cannot imagine. Perhaps the girl found it and then accidentally left it here in her moment of terror. As I stare at the crucifix, however, I am reminded of how this whole wretched nightmare began, and of the sliver of jealousy and greed that first began to crack open my soul.

CHAPTER TWENTY-TWO

"IF SHE KNOWS THAT we're here," the boy says as he and the new priest work in the office, "why doesn't she try to stop us?"

"Actually, I've been wondering that myself," he replies. "As demons go, Shaltak seems especially cautious."

"Did you hear that?" Shaltak purrs as I listen from the corridor. "He said my name. He has come to release me."

"So it's not actually Judith Prendergast?" the boy asks.

"It's her," he explains, "but she's still possessed by Shaltak."

"Again!" Shaltak enthuses, as the priest continues to speak. "I am recognized! After all this time trapped here with you, my name is still known out there in the world!"

"What are they going to do?" I whisper.

"There were times when I thought I'd be stuck here forever," Shaltak continues. "Actually, I think this period of enforced seclusion has been good for me. I have so many ideas for when I leave this place. By the end of this night, dear Judith, we shall say our farewells."

"No," I reply, "I won't let you. I'm strong enough to -"

Before I can finish, my left hand flinches and bangs against the wall.

"You were saying?" Shaltak chuckles. "I still have the power here."

"She *is* getting more confident, though," the priest says in the office, having evidently heard that little bump. "Seventy years is nothing to a demon."

"So what is a demon?" the boy asks after a moment. "You said its name is Shaltak, right? So who is Shaltak? What does she want?"

"Shaltak this, Shaltak that," the voice says in my mind. "It's like an orgy."

"They know about you," I point out. "That man is a priest. He'll stop you."

"He has a broken soul," she replies. "I don't know what happened, but I can sense his sorrow. Can't you, Judith? He has suffered a great loss and now he is keen. He is going to ask me for something in exchange for freeing me. Or, if he is particularly stupid, he'll free me and *then* ask. Either way, he'll end up dead and I'll end up walking away from this church."

"I'll warn the boy," I say, stepping back along the corridor as I try to think of something.

"And how will you do that? You don't even know how to make them see you."

"I'll find a way," I continue, before turning and hurrying to the door that leads upstairs. Grabbing the edge of the door, I slam it against the frame, but almost immediately I hear Shaltak laughing.

"Go ahead," she says, as I step back in shock, "you'll only make them work faster."

"Well," the priest says, and I turn to see that he has emerged from the office, "it looks like she slammed a door. How cliched for a ghost. I think maybe she's getting angry or nervous, but she's too afraid to strike at us directly. I'll have to -"

"I don't think I can do this," the boy says. "I'm sorry, man, but I'm no ghost-hunter or demon-hunter. This shit's starting to feel way too real and I want out."

As they argue, I try desperately to think of a way I might warn them. Shaltak would not have told me the truth not unless she was certain that her plan would work. I know she likes to torture me with these vile promises, but I still believe that there is a way to warn the priest and the boy. I hesitate for a moment longer, and then I turn just in time to see that the boy is hurrying to the main door.

"I'm not falling for any more of your games," he says, as I rush after him in a state of panic. "There's no way this is -"

Before I even know what I'm doing, I reach out and place a hand on his shoulder. I don't even expect him to notice, but he freezes in his tracks and after a moment I realize that in some way he must be able to sense me. I keep my hand in place and feel the warmth of his body.

"Shall I enter him?" Shaltak asks. "Shall I do to him, what I did to his friend? She died, you know. I can do the same thing to this boy."

"No," I whisper, staring at the back of the boy's head as I try to pull my hand away, only to find that Shaltak is holding it in place. "I won't let you."

"You can't stop me."

"I've stopped you doing things before."

"Then let me show you how it all works now."

Suddenly the boy turns and looks straight at me. Filled with fear, I realize that this might be my only chance to warn him, so I summon all my strength and lunge at him. As I do so, Shaltak tries to hold me back and I scream as I feel an immense pain in my head. Falling forward, I drop to the floor as the pain ripples through every fiber of my being.

Finally I manage to look up, and it is evident that the boy can no longer see me.

"Nice effort," Shaltak says, "but your warnings are futile. I can no longer be bothered to stop you. Within a few hours, Judith, I'll finally be free."

"Okay," the priest says to the boy, "I think you probably understand now that I was telling the truth. Are you ready to get this job done?"

***

"Shaltak."

Again the priest says that name as he reads at the altar, and again I feel Shaltak surging in my soul. I cry out as I try to restrain her, and after a few seconds I find that I'm just about able to keep her here. We're still in the corridor, and – ever since the priest began to read from his book – I've been struggling to keep Shaltak from going through to show herself.

"You can't keep this up forever," she whispers in my mind. "They're calling me, Judith. You've already lost."

Trying to ignore her gloating tones, I squeeze my eyes tight shut and focus on ensuring that she can't move my body. I don't know exactly what she's planning, but I can tell that she's drawn to the priest as he continues to read. Every time he says her name, Shaltak tries to burst forward and go to him, and it takes all my strength to hold her here. We're locked in a constant struggle, but as I squeeze my eyes even tighter I tell myself that I can restrain her. I just have to stay strong.

"Shaltak."

I let out a pained gasp as I feel Shaltak once again trying to twist forward. She turns first one way and then the other, and for a moment I fear that this might be when she succeeds. With my eyes still shut, I focus every last ounce of my strength on the task of holding her back, and finally I feel her sinking back a little. My mind is shaking with the effort that I just expended, but I'm already preparing for the next onslaught.

"You're pathetic," Shaltak says after a moment.

I refuse to respond. She's trying to weaken me.

"What do you think you're going to achieve?" she asks. "I've basically already won. You're an empty husk, Judith. It's time to surrender to the inevitable."

"Never!" I hiss, although I know it was a mistake to speak.

"You can't hold me back forever."

"You won't move an inch!" I snap.

"Oh no? I'm already in the archway, Judith."

"No," I reply, "you're -"

Suddenly I stop as I realize that the priest is still reading, and that his voice seems closer. Startled, I open my eyes and find to my horror that Shaltak wasn't lying. I thought I was holding her back, but while my eyes were closed she managed to get me to walk all the way along the corridor and through here to the arched doorway. Looking along the aisle, I see that the young boy is staring at me from over by the altar.

I scream, and in that instant I fall forward and land hard against the cold stone floor.

"Why did she do that?" the boy asks, before pausing for a moment. "Why did she scream? I mean, she's still got a mind, right? She still think. Did she just do it to scare us? She was way too far away for that. It doesn't make any fucking sense."

"Come on, Judith," Shaltak says as I try to turn and crawl away, "you know this is over now, don't you?"

"Never," I stammer, hauling myself to my feet and hurrying along the corridor, only to stop as I suddenly realize that Shaltak led me the wrong way.

I'm almost at the foot of the altar, and now I'm walking even though I want to turn and run.

"You'd better have something figured out," the boy says as I try to stop walking forward. "You've got more than a few books, yeah? Maybe it's time to sprinkle out some of that holy water."

Now I'm making my way up the steps.

“You have to run!” I shout at the boy, as I struggle to regain control of my body. “Get out of here! Both of you!”

Finally I summon the strength to lunge at him. I let out an agonized scream, but then I fall to my knees. My body is trembling and I can feel Shaltak laughing in my mind. She think she's on the verge of being released from this place, but I know I'll find a way to keep her here. The Lord is watching over us and will protect us in the end, no matter how bad things might seem now. As I struggle back to my feet, I try to regather my composure. Has Shaltak retreated a little from my mind? For a moment, I barely sense her at all.

“Do something!” the boy shouts at the priest. “Don't just stand there! You have to do something!”

He pauses.

“Liam!”

Suddenly Shaltak seizes control of me again and forces me to grab the side of the boy's neck. He freezes at my touch, but then slowly he turns and looks straight into my eyes.

“Liam,” he stammers, “please...”

“What are you doing in my church?” Shaltak asks, as if she's trying to goad him. She makes the words come from his mouth as well. “Who invited you here?”

He lets out a faint gasp.

"This is my church and you have no right to be here," Shaltak continues. "You must leave at once, you are not -"

Forcing her out of my mind, I let out a pained cry as I throw myself forward. I land hard against the side of the altar and then I stumble past the priest, who has now finally stopped reading from his book. For a moment I struggle to keep my thoughts together, and I can sense Shaltak's great appetite burning in my soul. She's savoring this moment, she's convinced that she's about to escape the church, and she thinks I'm powerless to stop her. I have to show her that she's wrong. And as the boy and the priest continue to talk, I realize that my only hope is to make them both understand that they're mixed up in something they can't possibly understand. I have to find a way to communicate with them. Slowly, I turn and step up behind the priest as I try to work out how I can make him hear me.

"Be ready," the priest says suddenly.

The boy begins to ask something, but then the priest turns and throws something at me.

Before I have a chance to realize what's happening, I feel an immense burning sensation rushing across my face. The pain is so great, I scream as I take a step forward, and then I stumble and have to stop so that I can support myself against the altar. The priest threw some kind of liquid at me, and I can feel a buzzing sensation rumbling all through my body.

"Nearly," Shaltak gasps excitedly. "Just a little more! It hurts so much, but the pain is a sign that the process is working!"

"What was that?" I stammer, as the pain begins to subside just a little.

Turning away from the altar, I step toward the priest once more. I have to find a way to make him understand what's happening. So long as he locks the church door and ensure it's never opened again, I can -

"There!" the boy shouts, suddenly pointing at me.

The priest throws more water at me, and this time the pain is even worse. I cry out in agony and turn away, and then I take a few faltering steps as I feel something slowly rising from my body.

"She's trapped," the priest says. "She knows she has to stop us now, but the holy water is wearing her down. One more time should be enough, but you have to remain vigilant. If she gets close to use again, we might not be able to fight her off. Mark, where is she now?"

"No, you're wrong," I gasp, stopping behind the altar and turning to them again as they continue to talk. "She wants you to do this! You're playing right into her -"

"There!" the boy shouts, pointing at me yet again.

I try to turn away, but the priest throws more of the water at me, this time hitting me in the center of the face. I scream as the pain burns through my mind, and then my knees buckle and I fall down against the stone floor. It feels different this time, and after a moment I realize I can sense a great weight starting to tear itself away from my soul. I can hear Shaltak laughing in my mind, but somehow her voice is becoming more distant, as if she's no longer a part of me.

"Thanks for the ride, Judith," she says with a sneer. "Enjoy oblivion."

"No!" I sob, as I realize that she's gone. I feel so empty without her, and I look around to see where she is now. When I realize that she's nowhere to be found, I break down into a series of heaving cries as I realize that I failed. I held on for so long, I managed to contain Shaltak, but the priest and the boy interfered and now Shaltak is loose. After all these years, she's free in the world and I am left behind to contemplate my failure.

"What's wrong with her?" the boy asks suddenly. "What happened?"

Looking up, I see that he and the priest are staring down at me. They look utterly shocked by my appearance, but I realize after a moment that maybe – just maybe – I still have a chance to warn them.

"No," I stammer as I try desperately to think of a way to explain, "please, you don't understand..."

"Don't let her get close to you," the priest says firmly, as he holds up a vial of water.

"Help me," I cry, reaching toward the boy. "I'm begging you..."

"Don't let her touch you!" the priest shouts.

"Please," I sob, "you have to help me! I'm so sorry for what I did, but you have to understand, I tried to hold her back! I tried to stop her! I was always -"

Hearing the priest stepping closer behind me, I realize that I have to hurry. I rush toward the boy, but the pain is intense and I scream. A moment later, the priest throws more of the water at me from behind, and the pain flares as I tilt my head back, and then everything goes dark.

CHAPTER TWENTY-THREE

“Mother, you can't give up now. You have to end this.”

CHAPTER TWENTY-FOUR

"SHE HAS TO BRING her back for me," the priest sobs as I open my eyes. "That's what all of this is for. She has to bring her back!"

For a moment, I don't even know who I am. I remember the pain, and then everything went dark and then even the darkness disappeared and there was nothing at all. I remember sinking out of existence, as if my mind was un-threading. And then...

"Elizabeth," I whisper, as I think back to the moment when I heard her voice.

It was really her.

She spoke to me as I slipped into the void, and something about her words made me come back. I remember who I am now, I remember sobbing, I remember the priest burning me with holy water and burning Shaltak too, and then Shaltak broke free.

"I bow down before you!" the priest shouts suddenly, and I turn to see that he's in a crumpled heap on the floor. "You're free now! You've been trapped in this church for more than seventy years, but now you can leave! You can do whatever you want in the world, and in return I ask only that you grant me the one thing that I need. Please, bring her back. I know she didn't just vanish into nothingness after she died. Her soul has to be somewhere. Bring her back, I -"

Suddenly a dark shape reaches down and grabs the priest by the throat, and I stare in shock as I see that this shape is a twisted, burned copy of my own body. I know instantly that this must be Shaltak in her new form, and I feel a shudder pass through my chest as I realize that she has taken my form. Perhaps she has no body of her own, or perhaps she is merely accustomed to the way I looked while she was inside me. There is an ugliness to her, however, and I can see the evil in her eyes as she grins and starts tearing at the priest's neck.

For a moment I can only watch with a growing sense of horror as Shaltak begins to twist the priest's head away from his neck, but then I turn and see that the boy is struggling to make his way out of the church. I know that the priest is a lost cause now, but in a flash I realize that the boy might yet be able to do something.

Racing along the aisle, I reach the boy just as he turns to look back at the priest. Screams are ringing out through the church, and I know I might only have a few seconds before I lose my final chance. At first I don't know what I can do, but then I see the wind and rain outside and in an instant I understand that Shaltak's fear of holy water might yet be turned against her.

"Water," I stammer, before turning to the boy. "You have to use holy water. It's the only thing that can stop her!"

I wait, but he doesn't seem to be able to hear me. He's simply watching with a horrified expression as Shaltak continues to decapitate the priest.

"You have to use holy water!" I scream, grabbing him by the shoulders. "Bless the water! It doesn't matter what water. You can even use the rain. Just bless it, there are no special words, you just have to have faith in something. Do you understand? Draw her out there and bless the rain!"

The boy hesitates, before turning and limping out of the church. I try to go after him, but I quickly find that I can't leave the church. Already, the boy is disappearing away into the darkness, and I still don't know whether he heard what I said to him just now.

"Bless the rain!" I shout after him. "You have to bless the rain!"

He's already gone. He didn't look at me while I was talking to him, but I tell myself that somehow – deep down – he must have heard me. He might not even have realized, but my words must have reached him. I just hope he realizes before it's too late.

"Judith Prendergast," a voice snarls behind me. "That's not *you*, is it?"

Turning, I see that Shaltak is standing in the arched doorway, holding the priest's head in one hand. Blood is dribbling from the severed neck, and a moment later the priest's decapitated body leans over and slumps down against the floor. Shaltak, meanwhile, is staring at me with a bemused expression, and a moment later a faint smile curls across those ravaged lips.

"Do you like the form I have taken?" she asks, holding her hands out and then dropping the head, letting it crunch down to the floor. "Inspired by you, with a few small changes here and there. I didn't want to copy your ugliness." She pauses. "But tell me, how are you here? I felt certain that you'd simply fade away once I was no longer anchoring you here. Very few humans have the strength to remain in this world after their bodies are gone."

"You won't succeed," I tell her.

"Succeed in what?"

"In whatever evil you're planning."

"And how do you work that out?" she asks.

"Because as demons go," I reply, "you don't seem very impressive. If demons could run amok in the world, one of them would have done it by now. Something must always hold you back."

"I'm sure you'd like to think so," she says, "but you're wrong about me. I'm by far the most impressive specimen of my kind."

"Again," I tell her, "I find that very difficult to believe."

"There's no point trying to delay me, you know," she continues, stepping toward me. "First I'm going to go and kill that pathetic boy, and then I think I'll have some fun in Briarwych. And while your continued existence might be rather irritating, it doesn't really change anything. You're still trapped here. Perhaps I'll burn the entire world and leave this church for last, so you can watch the flames and contemplate your role in it all."

"That won't happen," I reply.

"You know nothing."

"I know I heard my daughter's voice," I tell her, "just before it was all going to end."

"You're a romantic fool. Your daughter's soul died when her body died. In case you've forgotten what the world is like, Judith, there's not much hope out there. Bad things happen all the time, and where are the good things? There are barely any. Bad things always flourish. It's the bad that prospers."

"We only notice the bad thing," I reply, "because we're so used to all the good that surrounds us every day. The simple things, the complicated things, they're all out there. Sunrises, sunsets, love, hope, happiness, they're all part of the human condition. And maybe we don't notice them because we're so used to them, because we take them for granted. Meanwhile we notice the bad things precisely because they're so rare, because they stick out from everything else."

"I'm sure a -"

"And you'll never persuade me otherwise!" I snap, as I take a step toward her and stare into her cruel, evil face. "Nobody answered my prayers, because they didn't need answering. Because although there was a lot of pain and suffering, ultimately good will always triumph over evil."

"And you think you're going to stop me?" Shaltak asks with a smirk. "Is this going to be another tedious attempt to show your strength?"

"On the contrary," I reply, hesitating for a moment before stepping aside and gesturing toward the open doorway, "I don't need to stop you. In fact, I'm sick of the sound of your voice, so I'd be grateful if you could hurry up and leave this church. Something is waiting out there to stop you."

She opens her mouth to reply, but then I see a flicker of doubt in her eyes. She heard what I said and it's got to her, and her smirk has faded. She pauses, and then she mutters something angrily under her breath before storming past me and rushing out into the rain.

Taking a deep breath and hoping very much that I didn't just make a huge mistake, I watch as Shaltak disappears into the rain-ravaged night. I take a step forward and stop in the doorway, and I watch as the rain continues to fall. If I was wrong, then perhaps Shaltak will keep her promise and burn the world all around me, leaving me all alone here to watch it all. After a moment, however, I feel a flicker of hope in my heart, and I realize that I *wasn't* wrong. Creatures such as Shaltak will always cause minor trouble, and will always torment young girls they first spotted on warm days in the English countryside. They'll always exploit the weak and the foolish. But if the world was going to be ravaged by a demon, it would have happened by now, and it would have been caused by a far more powerful demon that the miserable Shaltak.

She will fail now that she is out of the church. Of that, I am certain.

EPILOGUE

Five years later

"I THOUGHT I RECOGNIZED you outside," Father Prior says as he continues to speak to the young man. "I trust that you're fully recovered from your injuries?"

"Completely."

"That's good to hear. I often wondered if you'd ever come back to see the place."

"I never planned to," the young man replies. "I don't even know why I came. I was just in the area, and I figured I should lay some ghosts to rest."

"I don't believe there *are* any ghosts here anymore."

"No, there aren't." The young man looks around for a moment. "I should go. I have a train to catch."

"Let me walk you out."

I watch as they head over to the door. I recognize the young man, he was here five years ago with that wretched priest who conducted the ceremony here in the church. He seems like a nice, gentle soul, and it is pleasing to hear that he recognizes a change in our lovely church. There is perhaps still a little way to go before the church has entirely recovered from the evil that once lurked here, but we shall get there in the end. And I cannot help but notice that the cemetery grass is looking particularly beautiful this morning. I certainly see nothing to suggest that a powerful demon has begun to ravage the world.

And then, suddenly, poor Amanda Lawley appears in the doorway.

"Mrs. Lawley," the priest says. "Is there any news about your dear husband?"

"There's no change," she tells him. "I thought I'd pray for a while."

"Of course."

Amanda Lawley heads through the arched doorway, and I immediately go after her. I can hear Father Prior talking to the young man, but I shall leave them to their conversation. After all, I have more pressing matters to which I must attend, so I follow Amanda along the aisle and then I watch as she sits in her usual position on one of the front pews. I, in turn, sit in *my* usual position on the pew directly behind.

"Lord," she whispers, sniffing back tears, "I feel so hopeless. Barry is still fighting, he's fighting hard, he's such a strong man. The doctors are hopeful, but I don't know how I can go on. Sometimes I want to just step out in front of the bus and end it all. I know that's wicked of me, but I simply don't have the strength to do this anymore. I'm scared I'm going to give up."

I listen for a moment as she sobs, and then – as I always do – I reach out and place a hand on her shoulder. She continues to sob for a few more seconds, before slowly raising her gaze and looking up toward the crucifix on the altar.

For the next few minutes, we sit in silence.

Finally, quite suddenly, Amanda gets to her feet and dabs at her eyes with a tissue, before making her way back long the aisle. This time I do not go with her. After all, I know that I have done what I needed to do today.

"If there is anything I can do to help," I hear Father Prior saying over by the door, "you must let me know."

"That's very kind of you," she replies. "You know, sometimes I genuinely feel that I can't go on. But then I come here, and I pray, and I sit for a short while, and somehow I don't feel so alone. Something about the church here gives me strength.

Is that strange?"

"Indeed it's not," he says, as they head outside. "You'd be surprised how many people tell me the exact same thing. This church has had a difficult history, but now it seems to be a source of great comfort."

Their voices fade into the distance, leaving me sitting here all alone in the church. I feel so desperately sorry for poor Amanda Lawley, and I wish I could do more to help her deal with her suffering. As it is, I can only be here for her and try to offer her some peace and calm, a role that I play for all the poor souls who come here for help. I sit with them, and I truly believe that in some ways they recognize my presence, even if they do not realize that I am truly here. Not that I require or even desire recognition, of course. I am just glad that after all the horrors that have befallen this beautiful place, we have weathered the storms and emerged with the ability to do some good.

That is my role here now, for I am – and shall always be – the ghost of Briarwych Church.

ALSO AVAILABLE

The Haunting of Briarwych Church
(The Briarwych Trilogy book 1)

The year is 1942. Britain is in the grip of the Second World War, bringing blackout conditions to much of the country. And in one of the country's oldest churches, a powerful evil begins to stir.

For several years, Briarwych Church has remained locked and unused. Arriving to take up his new position, Father Lionel Loveford's first task is to open the great wooden door and get the church back into use. But something lurks in the shadows. A terrible tragedy once took place in Briarwych, and now the locals live in fear of a vengeful spirit that has sometimes been spotted looking out from the church's windows.

Although he doesn't believe in ghosts, Father Loveford soon discovers that the entire village of Blackwych lives in a perpetual state of guilt and terror. Does the ghost of Judith Prendergast really haunt the church and, if so, what does she want from the villagers? With the door now unlocked, does her spirit now roam the village? And can her anger really reach as far as the wartorn fields of mainland Europe

?

ALSO AVAILABLE

The Horror of Briarwych Church
(The Briarwych Trilogy book 2)

Seventy years ago, Briarwych Church was sealed for the second time. The great wooden door has remained shut and locked ever since. But now, in the present day, evil is stirring once more.

Sent to live with new foster parents in Briarwych, Kerry and Mark soon set about exploring the village. When they're warned to stay away from the church, they naturally decide to go and take a closer look. And when the long-sealed door mysteriously swings open, they're drawn inside to meet a terrible fate.

After seventy years, a policy of containment is no longer enough. A priest is sent to Briarwych, with the sole task of defeating the evil once and for all. But what really lurks in the shadows of Briarwych Church? Why did Judith Prendergast turn to evil? And by attempting to banish the ghost forever, is Father Liam Dermott actually walking straight into an ancient and deadly trap?

BOOKS IN THIS SERIES

The Haunting of Briarwych Church
(The Briarwych Trilogy book 1)

The Horror of Briarwych Church
(The Briarwych Trilogy book 2)

The Ghost of Briarwych Church
(The Briarwych Trilogy book 3)

Also by Amy Cross

The Devil, the Witch and the Whore
(The Deal book 1)

"Leave the forest alone. Whatever's out there, just let it be. Don't make it angry."

When a horrific discovery is made at the edge of town, Sheriff James Kopperud realizes the answers he seeks might be waiting beyond in the vast forest. But everybody in the town of Deal knows that there's something out there in the forest, something that should never be disturbed. A deal was made long ago, a deal that was supposed to keep the town safe. And if he insists on investigating the murder of a local girl, James is going to have to break that deal and head out into the wilderness.

Meanwhile, James has no idea that his estranged daughter Ramsey has returned to town. Ramsey is running from something, and she thinks she can find safety in the vast tunnel system that runs beneath the forest. Before long, however, Ramsey finds herself coming face to face with creatures that hide in the shadows. One of these creatures is known as the devil, and another is known as the witch. They're both waiting for the whore to arrive, but for very different reasons. And soon Ramsey is offered a terrible deal, one that could save or destroy the entire town, and maybe even the world.

Also by Amy Cross

The Soul Auction

"I saw a woman on the beach. I watched her face a demon."

Thirty years after her mother's death, Alice Ashcroft is drawn back to the coastal English town of Curridge. Somebody in Curridge has been reviewing Alice's novels online, and in those reviews there have been tantalizing hints at a hidden truth. A truth that seems to be linked to her dead mother.

"Thirty years ago, there was a soul auction."

Once she reaches Curridge, Alice finds strange things happening all around her. Something attacks her car. A figure watches her on the beach at night. And when she tries to find the person who has been reviewing her books, she makes a horrific discovery.

What really happened to Alice's mother thirty years ago? Who was she talking to, just moments before dropping dead on the beach? What caused a huge rockfall that nearly tore a nearby cliff-face in half? And what sinister presence is lurking in the grounds of the local church?

Also by Amy Cross

Darper Danver: The Complete First Series

Five years ago, three friends went to a remote cabin in the woods and tried to contact the spirit of a long-dead soldier. They thought they could control whatever happened next. They were wrong...

Newly released from prison, Cassie Briggs returns to Fort Powell, determined to get her life back on track. Soon, however, she begins to suspect that an ancient evil still lurks in the nearby cabin. Was the mysterious Darper Danver really destroyed all those years ago, or does her spirit still linger, waiting for a chance to return?

As Cassie and her ex-boyfriend Fisher are finally forced to face the truth about what happened in the cabin, they realize that Darper isn't ready to let go of their lives just yet. Meanwhile, a vengeful woman plots revenge for her brother's murder, and a New York ghost writer arrives in town to uncover the truth. Before long, strange carvings begin to appear around town and blood starts to flow once again.

Also by Amy Cross

The Ghost of Molly Holt

"Molly Holt is dead. There's nothing to fear in this house."

When three teenagers set out to explore an abandoned house in the middle of a forest, they think they've found the location where the infamous Molly Holt video was filmed.

They've found much more than that...

Tim doesn't believe in ghosts, but he has a crush on a girl who does. That's why he ends up taking her out to the house, and it's also why he lets her take his only flashlight. But as they explore the house together, Tim and Becky start to realize that something else might be lurking in the shadows.

Something that, ten years ago, suffered unimaginable pain.

Something that won't rest until a terrible wrong has been put right.

Also by Amy Cross

American Coven

He kidnapped three women and held them in his basement. He thought they couldn't fight back. He was wrong...

Snatched from the street near her home, Holly Carter is taken to a rural house and thrown down into a stone basement. She meets two other women who have also been kidnapped, and soon Holly learns about the horrific rituals that take place in the house. Eventually, she's called upstairs to take her place in the ice bath.

As her nightmare continues, however, Holly learns about a mysterious power that exists in the basement, and which the three women might be able to harness. When they finally manage to get through the metal door, however, the women have no idea that their fight for freedom is going to stretch out for more than a decade, or that it will culminate in a final, devastating demonstration of their new-found powers.

Also by Amy Cross

The Ash House

Why would anyone ever return to a haunted house?

For Diane Mercer the answer is simple. She's dying of cancer, and she wants to know once and for all whether ghosts are real.

Heading home with her young son, Diane is determined to find out whether the stories are real. After all, everyone else claimed to see and hear strange things in the house over the years. Everyone except Diane had some kind of experience in the house, or in the little ash house in the yard.

As Diane explores the house where she grew up, however, her son is exploring the yard and the forest. And while his mother might be struggling to come to terms with her own impending death, Daniel Mercer is puzzled by fleeting appearances of a strange little girl who seems drawn to the ash house, and by strange, rasping coughs that he keeps hearing at night.

The Ash House is a horror novel about a woman who desperately wants to know what will happen to her when she dies, and about a boy who uncovers the shocking truth about a young girl's murder.

Also by Amy Cross

Haunted

Twenty years ago, the ghost of a dead little girl drove Sheriff Michael Blaine to his death.

Now, that same ghost is coming for his daughter.

Returning to the small town where she grew up, Alex Roberts is determined to live a normal, quiet life. For the residents of Railham, however, she's an unwelcome reminder of the town's darkest hour.

Twenty years ago, nine-year-old Mo Garvey was found brutally murdered in a nearby forest. Everyone thinks that Alex's father was responsible, but if the killer was brought to justice, why is the ghost of Mo Garvey still after revenge?

And how far will the real killer go to protect his secret, when Alex starts getting closer to the truth?

Haunted is a horror novel about a woman who has to face her past, about a town that would rather forget, and about a little girl who refuses to let death stand in her way.

Also by Amy Cross

The Curse of Wetherley House

"If you walk through that door, Evil Mary will get you."

When she agrees to visit a supposedly haunted house with an old friend, Rosie assumes she'll encounter nothing more scary than a few creaks and bumps in the night. Even the legend of Evil Mary doesn't put her off. After all, she knows ghosts aren't real. But when Mary makes her first appearance, Rosie realizes she might already be trapped.

For more than a century, Wetherley House has been cursed. A horrific encounter on a remote road in the late 1800's has already caused a chain of misery and pain for all those who live at the house. Wetherley House was abandoned long ago, after a terrible discovery in the basement, something has remained undetected within its room. And even the local children know that Evil Mary waits in the house for anyone foolish enough to walk through the front door.

Before long, Rosie realizes that her entire life has been defined by the spirit of a woman who died in agony. Can she become the first person to escape Evil Mary, or will she fall victim to the same fate as the house's other occupants?

Also by Amy Cross

The Ghosts of Hexley Airport

Ten years ago, more than two hundred people died in a horrific plane crash at Hexley Airport.

Today, some say their ghosts still haunt the terminal building.

When she starts her new job at the airport, working a night shift as part of the security team, Casey assumes the stories about the place can't be true. Even when she has a strange encounter in a deserted part of the departure hall, she's certain that ghosts aren't real.

Soon, however, she's forced to face the truth. Not only is there something haunting the airport's buildings and tarmac, but a sinister force is working behind the scenes to replicate the circumstances of the original accident. And as a snowstorm moves in, Hexley Airport looks set to witness yet another disaster.

Also by Amy Cross

The Girl Who Never Came Back

Twenty years ago, Charlotte Abernathy vanished while playing near her family's house. Despite a frantic search, no trace of her was found until a year later, when the little girl turned up on the doorstep with no memory of where she'd been.

Today, Charlotte has put her mysterious ordeal behind her, even though she's never learned where she was during that missing year. However, when her eight-year-old niece vanishes in similar circumstances, a fully-grown Charlotte is forced to make a fresh attempt to uncover the truth.

Originally published in 2013, the fully revised and updated version of *The Girl Who Never Came Back* tells the harrowing story of a woman who thought she could forget her past, and of a little girl caught in the tangled web of a dark family secret.

Also by Amy Cross

Asylum
(The Asylum Trilogy book 1)

"No-one ever leaves Lakehurst. The staff, the patients, the ghosts... Once you're here, you're stuck forever."

After shooting her little brother dead, Annie Radford is sent to Lakehurst psychiatric hospital for assessment. Hearing voices in her head, Annie is forced to undergo experimental new treatments devised by a mysterious old man who lives in the hospital's attic. It soon becomes clear that the hospital's staff, led by the vicious Nurse Winter, are hiding something horrific at Lakehurst.

As Annie struggles to survive the hospital, she learns more about Nurse Winter's own story. Once a promising young medical student, Kirsten Winter also heard voices in her head. Voices that traveled a long way to reach her. Voices that have a plan of their own. Voices that will stop at nothing to get what they want.

What kind of signals are being transmitted from the basement of the hospital? Who is the old man in the attic? Why are living human brains kept in jars? And what is the dark secret that lurks at the heart of the hospital?

Also by Amy Cross

The Devil's Hand

"I felt it last night! I was all alone, and suddenly a hand touched my shoulder!"

The year is 1943. Beacon's Ash is a private, remote school in the North of England, and all its pupils are fallen girls. Pregnant and unmarried, they have been sent away by their families. For Ivy Jones, a young girl who arrived at the school several months earlier, Beacon's Ash is a nightmare, and her fears are strengthened when one of her classmates is killed in mysterious circumstances.

Has the ghost of Abigail Cartwright returned to the school? Who or what is responsible for the hand that touches the girls' shoulders in the dead of night? And is the school's headmaster Jeremiah Kane just a madman who seeks to cause misery, or is he in fact on the trail of the Devil himself? Soon ghosts are stalking the dark corridors, and Ivy realizes she has to face the evil that lurks in the school's shadows.

The Devil's Hand is a horror novel about a girl who seeks the truth about her friend's death, and about a madman who believes the Devil stalks the school's corridors in the run-up to Christmas.

For more information, visit:

www. amycross.com

Made in the USA
Columbia, SC
22 April 2022

59339165R00186